A WAY TO GO

by

Alan Melzak

Also by Alan Melzak:

The Amaranthine Triangle

Black Magenta

Deadly Likeness

Deathrun

Dual Purpose

Earthsigh

The Enchantress

The Keating Legacy

Lifeline

A Matter of Fancy

Mindprint

Skindeep

Chapters

1. The Man Has a Better Way — 7
2. Devils Night Out — 33
3. Expedition Anonymous — 73
4. Apache Warrior — 104
5. Death by Drowning — 124
6. Eyes Like a Cat — 146
7. Dead Men Hanging — 168
8. Cabin Fever — 195
9. Cards on the Table — 222
10. Retrieval — 245

ONE: THE MAN HAS A BETTER WAY

The Mexican cop braked to a halt, grabbed my wrist and uncuffed me. I was sitting up front next to him. The car, a Ford Pickup with *San Petro Policia* painted on the doors, had reached the end of an unused track, a turning that led off the highway that two weeks earlier had brought me to the town. The journey over the pitted crumbling surface had taken the best part of an hour. It was still early morning though, the sky cloudless. Through the dusty windscreen I had a view of flat scrubland fading to a misty horizon, the darker grey broken, the outline of a mountainous range.

The jailhouse cop took out his pack of cigarettes. "*Estamos aqui, hijo.*"

I frowned. There was no sign or indication that we had reached the US border. "Which direction do you want me to take?" I asked.

"*En espanol, por favor.*"

"Okay." At times the cop insisted I speak to him in Spanish. "*Donde esta California?*"

He pointed into the far-off mistiness. "*El norte.*"

We sat there smoking together for a while. His name was Pepe and he had always treated me considerately - I guess because I was young, seventeen years old.

The deal they offered me was either wait for the magistrate or else pay a fifty-dollar fine and leave the country. I chose to wait. It was a minor misdemeanour, and fifty-seven bucks was all they found on me, all the money I had. But after fourteen days in the jailhouse, often sharing the cell with drunks, I gave up on the good nature of a wandering magistrate.

"I take it you split the fifty bucks with the others," I said on the journey in the car.

Pepe sighed. "If you want, I give you back my share."

"No, keep the money. Payment for the lessons." In those two weeks my Spanish had come on close to fluent.

Stepping out of the car, I had a clear sight of the abandoned building glimpsed through the dusty windscreen, an arched doorway with windows on either side like empty eye-sockets. Now I saw that a huge wooden cross stood high above on a partly intact slanted roof. "Is that a church way out here, Pepe?" I asked.

"*Si. La Iglesia de los Muertos.*"

The Church of the Dead? Shit man. No wonder the place is deserted."

Pepe spread his arms. "The land was not always like this. Once it was open range and farming country. Look, I show you." He brought a faded photograph of the church from his wallet, intact, set amongst trees, with people in the frame. "My family come from here."

I looked closer. Men like him, strolling, dressed in their Sunday best. "What happened then?"

"Visitors brought a plague. Everything dried up and died. Now nobody come. They think the church is bad luck."

"Superstition," I said.

"*Si,*" he agreed, and crossed himself.

I handed back the photo. "Why did you do that?"

"Because we both might be wrong."

He put the photo back in his wallet and reached into the rear of the Ford Pickup for my backpack. The label dangling from the rolled up sleeping bag read 'Jon'. I spelled my name that way because the unpronounced 'H' seemed as irrelevant as my life.

He removed the label and helped me on with the backpack. "Listen, inside you find water and food."

I turned to face him, offering my hand. "Thanks, *compadre*."

The Mexican cop gripped my arm instead. "*Vaya con dios*, Bad weather is coming."

I had heard the weather report on the car radio. It was in Spanish, but I understood enough to know a major storm was on its way inland.

I set off, not turning until I heard the noise of a car horn. He waved at me through the open window, gave a final beep, and drove off. I was alone once again.

The terrain was rock and sand, with an occasional patch of weedy growth, or a cluster of cacti. My eyes picked out a ridge or spur ahead as a spot to reach, the direction to go. My pace scarcely slackened, fuelled by a sense of freedom.

The first flurry of snow came on the forest's edge. The sky, arace with black low clouds, had darkened into near night, it was like watching the opening scene of an old black and white horror movie. At midday I had sheltered from the blazing sun in a shady spot, dozing in the heat. Now I shivered in a gusting wind, my tee-shirt and jeans still damp from sweat. The suddenness of the change was hard to believe.

Reaching further into the trees, the wind died down a little. I put on the black leather jacket folded in the backpack, zipping it to the top. A surprise awaited me. Along with my last seven bucks, the cop had left a pack of Mexican cigarettes and a gas lighter in the pockets. I waited until I had unrolled the sleeping bag and climbed in, my head against a tree, before lighting up.

My thoughts turned to the day I arrived at San Petro. Was the visit by chance, or was it predestined by a Master Operator? I was never certain of any of the twists and turns I had made in life. At any rate, the driver in the Durango coach park nodded when I asked, "Is this okay for California?" I was heading back to LA, my money almost gone. By then I'd spent several weeks in Mexico, hitching lifts, catching buses. Travelling alone was not a problem for me, I lived inside myself, my mind active with inner dialogue.

The journey to San Petro lasted ten hours, mostly through the night. I was the only passenger left in the coach. The driver opened the door for me. This time I spoke Spanish. *"Estamos en California?"*

"No, San Petro."

I stepped out, not giving him the dollar bill in my hand.

Wandering around in darkness the place seemed orderly but nondescript, a small town with a few bars, a cinema, a hotel, a police station. At midday I was taken in by a cop for sleeping on a municipal bench. Pepe was the jailhouse *sargento*, the closest I came to making a friend in Mexico.

I took a last puff of tobacco smoke and flicked the cigarette butt away. The sleeping bag had a hood. Pulling it down, covering my face, I closed my eyes. Sleep came easily to me, my body was fatigued and in need of recuperation.

The coldness of dawn woke me. My eyes opened to a desolate scene. The wind had whipped up into a gale, the snow flurries had become a blizzard. A drift against the tree covered my sleeping bag. Lying there, shivering, I almost wished I was looking up at a patch of blue sky through a barred window and hearing the rattle of Pepe opening the cell door for breakfast.

At length I wriggled out of the sleeping bag and reached across for the backpack. My jacket and shoes were dry, stowed inside, but first I put on extra socks, a second t-shirt, a sweater. Warmer now, hunger took hold of me.

Pepe's tortilla had gone stale. I ate every crumb of it and swallowed the last mouthful of water, all that remained in the litre bottle after crossing the scrubland. Standing sheltered by the tree against the gale, I smoked another cigarette.

The trees were thin and sparse at the forest edge, no barrier against the driving blizzard. Deeper in, I figured the trees would provide greater protection. I set off trying to avoid the drifts that had accumulated in the hollows, apart from the one where I refilled the water bottle with snow. Using a broken tree branch as a walking stick to guide me, I was forced to zig-zag and back-track, losing any sense of direction I might have had. Here deep in the forest with no sight of the sun, for all I knew I might be moving in a circle and return to where I began.

Eventually I became aware that the ground sloped. A memory of the darker grey of a mountainous range beyond the forest came to me bringing back my lost sense of direction. The route I chose was upward.

The nature of the forest changed as I moved deeper. The trees became larger and taller, oaks and elms separated from each other, the ground between matted by fallen leaves, twigs, and branches. And there were the sights and sounds of animal life, broken nutshells left by squirrels, the call of birds. I stayed alert for any movement, or track, that might come from a bear or a wolf or a man.

In late afternoon, the setting sun cast long shadows in the forest and, looking up, patches of blue sky showed above. The wind still gusted flurries of snow and, here and there, I came upon slippery patches of ice, but the drifts were gone. It seemed I had climbed beyond the bad weather.

My eyes caught a faint movement. A few paces away a rabbit emerged from a burrow. I was lightning fast, a born hunter. A blow from the stick shattered the furry animal's skull.

I chose a spot close by an elm tree where the ground had dried. Gathering leaves and twigs I started with a small fire, adding branches, waiting until the embers glowed. I had skinned the rabbit with my knife and prepared a tripod of sticks. I laid the carcass on the tripod and watched it roast. I ate sparsely. The rabbit, though large, was scrawny, enough food for two meals at most. Afterwards I lay down and watched the smoke curl up to a piece of night sky that showed above.

Awakening next morning my lips felt cracked and sore to my tongue, my mouth dry as the desert I had crossed. A rabbit emerged from the undergrowth and watched me swallow the last few drops of melted snow that remained in the bottle. They did nothing to quench my thirst. The rabbit scuttled into its burrow as I approached, my eyes had picked out an opening in the undergrowth beyond. I followed the tell-tale signs left by small animals – bent grass, paw prints, dung - a track that led to a shallow crystal-clear stream. I stood knee-deep in the middle scooping water into my mouth, filling the bottle to the brim. On the far bank, amongst the footprints of small animals, deeper imprints showed, the encrusted shapes made by shoes.

I followed the shoe prints - they appeared to be light moccasins - to the rear of a log cabin. My manner became stealthy. Circling round to the front I saw that the cabin lay on the edge of a substantial clearing. The log roof sloped down over a porch, a door, and a window. The porch and the door were smooth, made of wood planks, the window a thick pane of glass without a handle or a hinge. Peering through the glass pane there was no sign of anyone living inside. Solitary by nature, I felt relieved.

A growl from the undergrowth made me freeze. The animal was unseen, but I recognized the sound. Not a bear nor a wolf, but a dog. A large one, judging by the deep rumble

I crossed the clearing to the far edge, a hundred paces or more. There I spotted the moccasin prints again. They led to a trodden-down trail that wound between the trees. In some way it gave me a sense of direction. Though mostly in semi-gloom, from time to time a ray of sunlight penetrated the canopy of foliage. And then, with startling suddenness, sunshine blinded me. I had entered an area open to the sky.

Shading my eyes, I saw that a massive tree trunk lay at the centre. A tree which must have brought down several others when it fell, accounting for the open sky above. Clearly an event that had happened years before, for there was no evidence of fallen trees, they had rotted away, only the massive tree trunk remained.

The sun was almost directly overhead. It seemed the right moment to stop and eat. I heaved myself up onto the trunk, taking care to eat only half of what remained of the rabbit. Afterwards I lit a cigarette.

Sitting there, smoking, I rapped on the tree trunk with my knuckles. I remember the sound it gave, hollow, like an empty wooden box. Soon, though, my attention was taken by another, the drone of an airplane. The sound grew louder, became deafening. I looked up. An instant of darkness as a black shadow passed across the opening, leaving a trail of black smoke drifting down in the sunlight. Moments later I heard a ripping tearing noise that told me the plane had crashed into the forest.

I followed the direction the shadow had taken. The plane had travelled a distance after passing over me, a mile at the least. It lay upended at the base of a tree, a jagged gash torn in the forest canopy above. Smoke blurred the scene but neither the engine nor the fuselage was aflame. Coming closer I saw a coating of thick black ice on the wings of the plane, the weight causing it to lose height.

I could see two occupants inside the cabin, the door had burst open. The pilot was hanging by his straps. His sunglasses were intact, his eyes staring sightlessly through the lenses. The passenger was crumpled, eyes closed, in the other seat, his head at an unnatural angle. There was no need for me to enter or to check, they were both dead.

Sickened, I closed the cabin door and turned away. To my surprise, a suitcase was lying on the ground a few paces from the plane. I crouched down. The case was large, dark brown, made of thick hide leather, heavy-looking. The catches sprang open easily. I lifted the lid expecting to see the belongings of a well-off traveller starting out on a lengthy trip. Instead, the inside was packed tight with rows of polythene packets filled with a whitish powder.

I closed the lid and sat cross-legged on the suitcase. The two dead men were drug traffickers. I was alone in the wilderness sitting on a haul of cocaine worth a million bucks or more. It was too good an opportunity to miss. And in my experience the police were not to be trusted with the haul anyway.

I lifted the suitcase. It was too heavy and cumbersome to take with me. And too dangerous. But leaving the coke there for somebody else to find was not an option. I moved off retracing my footsteps. I had in mind a place in which to hide the case.

The following day the nature of the forest changed again, the trees became evergreens, towering pines and spruce, heavy with dark green foliage, shutting out whatever lay above and beyond. The weather had stayed wintery but now the ground was hard with frost, the incline steeper, and somehow snow was finding a way through. It was tiring but I kept going.

Around noon the forest straggled away giving me a view of what lay ahead. Sunlight glistened on two snow covered mountains but lower down where there was no snow, I picked out what seemed to be a track, one that I figured must lead to a pass between the two high peaks.

The path vanished under the snow, but I continued to climb, my eyes fixed on the gap that separated the mountains. A long hard ascent that ended at the mouth of a pass. Dusk had come. I made a small fire from twigs gathered in the forest, warming myself, smoking the last of the Mexican cigarettes. There was no food, the remains of the rabbit had been my breakfast. Before sliding unto the sleeping bag, I opened my backpack. The packet of cocaine taken from the suitcase and wrapped in a used t-shirt, was intact, the cellophane unbroken. Coming from the City of Angels, I knew where and how to sell coke.

I grew up in a boarding house in downtown LA, a place run by my grandmother. She had been a bit part player in Hollywood movies back in the late 1940's, which made her at the very least in her eighties, though you'd never guess her that old in her glamorous make-up and her offkey behaviour. Her daughter, my mother, was a jazz singer. I have vague memories of her, the last one of a tousle-haired brunette who gave me and my sister a hug and a kiss before leaving us with grandma. I was aged four, my sister was seven.

I have no knowledge of my father. The best I can get is that he was a musician.

"Was that my pa with her, gran?" I asked, aged ten. We were talking about the night she left us.

"No, certainly not, Johnny."

Ellie was my half-sister. "Was he Ellie's pa?"

"Good heavens, no." My grandmother shuddered. "That big ugly man was your mother's sandman."

Ellie was listening. She told me that *sandman* was her word for a dope pedlar.

I slept soundly in the mountain pass, waking at sunrise. Lying there it took me a while to remember where I was. But when I did, my intention became clear. What lay beyond the mountains was unknown but, somehow, I needed to find my way back to Los Angeles. I dressed and gathered my belongings. Ready to leave, a sudden premonition took hold of me, the kind you get at night walking alone down an empty unlit street. Screwing my eyes against the glare of sunlight on the snow, my gaze tracked back to the forest, to a tiny moving figure, though whether man or beast was impossible to tell.

The pass led down to a river gorge. The mountain water that rushed through had frozen solid. Reaching the other side, I looked back up at the high peak. The tiny figure glimpsed from the mouth of the pass was a man, I had sight of him now high on the mountainside. My premonition of danger had been a warning, I was being pursued.

Earlier, coming down from the pass, I had a view of scrubland stretching beyond the mountain. It was a desolate plateau littered with rocks and boulders, some of them head high. I climbed one and saw that the man in pursuit had gained on me. I jumped down, quickening my pace.

From far off I caught a sound familiar to me, the rumble of a truck travelling fast along an open highway. I broke into a run and reached the highway in time to see the truck surge by. I watched it become smaller in the distance and finally disappear. The road was bare and empty in both directions. I stayed there on the roadside waiting for another vehicle to appear, something I had done many times before. Walking along the highway or beyond the highway was not an option, the last of my energy had been used up in the run. I felt weak and hungry.

After a while, and with the highway still empty in both directions, I had recovered enough strength to climb up a boulder a few paces away. The view from there showed the man loping towards me, much closer than before, close enough for me to see that he wore a hat and carried a rifle slung across his back. At the same instant I heard a high-pitched squeal. A glance revealed a car a mile or more away moving at top speed in my direction from the south.

I scrambled from the boulder and stepped into the middle of the highway, raising my arms. The car, a Pontiac Firebird, lemon-green in colour, slammed on its brakes and came to a standstill alongside me.

The driver lowered the window. A big man, his open-neck shirt and his slacks were as colourful as the car. A forefinger pushed up his gold-rimmed sunglasses. "Shit, boy! Is somebody chasing you?"

"Yeah. I've got no idea why."

"Listen, I ain't asking why. Is he a white mother-fucker is what I wanna know?"

"Yeah. And he's carrying a rifle."

"In that case you just got yourself a ride, brother."

I climbed in, closing the door.

The Pontiac accelerated forward. "Is that the guy?"

My pursuer had come out onto the highway, he was shielding his eyes with a hand, gazing in our direction, his face unseen under the wide-brimmed hat. "Yeah, that's him, alright."

"Are you a stranger around here?"

I nodded. "Just passing through, that's all."

"This is New Mexico, kid. They ain't too friendly in these parts."

A road sign came up a few minutes later. The driver spat through the window. "Heronimo Town. Is that chicken shit dump okay with you?"

"That depends on where you are headed."

"Man, you ain't talking to no bone poor trash here. I ain't stopping nowhere till I hit L.A."

"That's cool, man. I've never been there before."

He pulled into the first gas station we came to on the highway past Heronimo town, the tank was close to empty. His name was Kilton. "Here, go get me a coffee and donut, and whatever you fancy eating and drinking."

I took his ten-dollar bill and spent it on two coffees, two donuts, and a ham sandwich, leaving the rest, about fifty cents, as a tip.

Kilton was waiting for me behind the wheel. He drove one handed, the other hand holding the coffee, the needle hovering in the mid-seventies. He kept pretty much to that speed all the way. "Kid, they always got cops looking for trouble. And to them a guy like me in a car like this means trouble."

"Don't you need a break from driving?" I asked. We were in Arizona.

He grunted. "Listen there ain't nothing worth stopping for this side of California."

A few hours later we reached Los Angeles. The dashboard clock showed nine-forty-five, night had fallen. "Kid," he said, "if you've got no place to sleep, I got a couch you can use."

I had lied to KIlton. Like I said, I knew LA well, I was raised there. But I had a plan in mind, one in which nobody would know me or my whereabouts. "Thanks for the offer," I told him, "but I've got a pal who'll put me up."

He dropped me off outside a shopping mall still open in downtown LA. I spent three of my last seven dollars on a package of polythene grip seal bags, the rest on a beer in a saloon bar nearby. Locking myself in the men's toilet, I doled a little coke into several of the seal grip bags.

From there I made my way to a down-at-heel shopping street close to South Park. The shops were closed, but I knew people went there late at night to buy drugs. The spot I chose was at the top of a dark narrow alley that led off the street.

A car slowed and a figure stepped out of a shop doorway. I waited until the driver shook his head before showing myself. The car pulled in. The driver, a young guy with a girl, lowered the window. "What have you got?"

"What do you want?"

"Coke."

"I got some."

He looked at the girl. She nodded. "Okay. Two hits."

"A hundred and forty bucks."

He took the bag of coke, handed me the dollar bills, and drove off.

It was a method of dealing that suited me. Sometimes the car drove on past me but whenever one slowed, I made sure I had a sale. When they asked the price, I said 'the usual', and took whatever they offered me.

About an hour past midnight, a police car cruised by. The sidewalk emptied, the figures in shop doorways gone. I left, too, my pockets stuffed with money. I used some to pay for a room at a cheap hotel nearby. I counted how much remained on the bed. Twelve hundred and ten dollars. I slept badly, kept awake by noises I had become unused to, like creaking pipes and slamming doors.

Next day I moved to a decent hotel, one of a chain of franchises, and stayed in my room until all the coke was parcelled into the polythene bags. Later I rented a box in a depository several streets away, leaving my backpack there, along with half the packaged coke. By my calculation, the total street value of the coke was almost twenty thousand dollars, and all I needed was maybe seven or eight thousand. The way I figured the future, it was unlikely that I'd ever be back for the rest. But I returned to the downtown shopping mall to buy a fresh backpack and sleeping bag, and road maps of New Mexico and the two states I needed to cross to get there, California and Arizona.

My intention was to sell enough coke to buy a car, drive to *La Iglesia de los Muertos*, arriving at night, leave the car inside the church, and then retrace my footsteps to where the suitcase was hidden.

In my mind I re-did the trek I had made through the desert and the forest over and over. I remembered every step of the way. Two and a half days at most to get there.

Heading back to the car might take a little longer. The backpack was large enough to hold all the packs of cocaine, and the extra load, even without the leather suitcase, might tire me, slow me down. Even so, my expectation was to be back at the church that nobody attended five nights after I set out from it. I pictured myself driving off in moonlight, leaving in a cloud of dust.

After that I had no clear plan or vision. Just hit the road to freedom.

My only worry was that someone would recognise me dealing on the street. A small chance because the people who knew me came from the boarding house where I was raised, elderly Hollywood people, the type who would not want to be seen dead in any dubious locality.

Buying a car was not a problem, though it wasn't the Pontiac Firebird I had pictured. The owner took my dollars and asked no questions. Five days had passed, I was still a thousand dollars short, the car and the hotel bill had taken most of my money.

I parked the car, a Ford saloon, at the end of the alley, intending to leave in time to arrive at the ruined church at nightfall. Most of the coke had been sold, the rest was in a shopping bag at my feet. I pocketed a handful of the bags, all that was needed, a grands-worth, and dumped the rest in a refuse bin in the alley.

I had moved my regular position to the shopping street a few paces from the alley. Guys who liked my stuff came back looking for me. Standing in a doorway, a black saloon came into my view. It slowed and pulled up. I sauntered over. It was past midnight, all I had left were three bags, this could be my final customer

Two men were sitting up front. The guy next to the driver lowered the window. He was the older of the two, a man with a grey crewcut. "Are you lost?" I asked.

"That depends. Are you Jon?"

I felt myself tighten inside when he spoke my name. Both men were unknown to me. On the other hand, satisfied customers had wanted to know who I was, and perhaps passed my name on. I stayed cagey, though. "It could be."

His face wrinkled into a frown. "What is this, kid, some kind of guessing game? Are you him, or ain't you?"

I saw the driver start to get out. "Yeah, that's me." I raised my hand. "Hold on a minute. Money first."

The older man sighed. "Isn't it sad. The kid doesn't trust you."

The driver handed some banknotes to him which he passed to me through the window. I counted them, four one hundred-dollar bills. I put the money in a jacket pocket. "Your pal stays in the car. Okay?"

"Sure, I get it. You don't trust him."

He climbed out of the car and followed me into the alley. I reached into the refuse bin and brought out three bags of coke. I added the ones in my pocket and offered them to him.

"Is that all I get for four hundred bucks?"

"Hey, it's the best. Pure, uncut."

The grey-haired man took one of the bags from me. He was bigger than he looked sitting in the car. "That sounds okay. But my pal doesn't trust anybody." He opened the polythene bag. "Not even me."

I watched him taste the white powder.

He gave a nod and sealed the grip. "How many bags of the shit have you got?"

"I haven't counted."

"Take a guess."

"About ten more hits."

"Is that all?"

I played cagey again. "How much do you want?"

The man looked hard at me. "I'm talking twenty kilos."

A warning bell rang. I ducked my head, shuffled my feet. "Listen, you have got me wrong, man. I only deal small time."

"Maybe so. But the trouble you are in right now is kind of big time."

"Yeah? How big?"

"That's up to you, kid."

"I guess you must be a cop."

"Yeah, Lake is the name. And the guy waiting in the car is detective Berns."

I thrust my hands forward. "Aren't you going to cuff me?"

"Like I said, kid, that is up to you."

"I guess you want me to make a run for it."

"Now why would I want you to do that?"

"I don't know. Get me for avoiding arrest maybe. Make yourself look bigger and braver."

He sighed and brought out a pair of handcuffs: I ducked past him and ran down the alley. Detective Berns was waiting at the far end, leaning against his car, blocking the way. I kept running and leaped forward onto the roof of the car. Berns grabbed at me. I lost my balance and fell, sprawling on the ground.

"What's your hurry, kid?"

I lifted my head and saw Berns grinning down at me. Lake reached us. "I'll make the call." He turned away to use his mobile phone.

Berns jerked me to my feet. He was bigger than his partner, and uglier. "Start singing. Where do you keep the rest of the stash?"

"All I got left is a few more hits. They are in the alley, in a rubbish bin. Ask your pal, he knows which bin. Or if you want, I'll go get them."

Berns bunched his fist. "Time for a lesson, punk. I don't play guessing games."

I saw Lake make a negative gesture at Berns and toss the handcuffs to him, he was listening to someone on the phone. Berns shoved me face forward over the car. I heard the snap of the handcuffs around my wrists. He pushed me into the car at the back and slammed the door shut.

Lake pocketed the phone and came over to Berns waiting at the driver door. The window was open, and I heard Berns ask, "Are you going soft, partner?"

Lake shrugged. "Beating up on a juvenile isn't smart. The Man says he's got a better way."

They both climbed into the front of the car, Berns behind the wheel.

TWO: DEVILS NIGHT OUT

Leem caught up with them, he was panting. "Please, Miss. How…how much further do we have to go?"

Eileen Porter managed to keep her tone bright. "My word Leem, you came just in time. Take a peep." She pointed. "We are here, at the top of Merlin's Loaf."

The boy sighed and slumped down on a flat rock for a breather. She made allowance for him however, he was barely sixteen, skinny and pasty-faced.

The other two youngsters followed her to the cliff edge. A Welsh valley lay a sheer drop several hundred feet below, a snow-capped mountain rising beyond.

"Sort of awesome, isn't it?" Fara said. She was aged sixteen like Leem but acted far more grown up.

Rees was seventeen, a year older. He grunted. "Is this why you brought us here, Miss? To see the view?"

"Oh dear, you are not impressed, are you, Rees?" she said, as if disappointed.

"No, I ain't. The way you was talking all this up, it don't match. You spot me?"

Eileen sighed. "It seems I must have exaggerated a little."

She had told them in the minibus that they were her special pick, which they were though not for the reason they supposed, a reward for good behaviour. On the contrary, they were notable for being the reverse, uncooperative, at times downright disobedient. As a psychotherapist who specialised in the treatment of adolescent offenders, they were the hardest challenge to her methods that she could find at the Institute.

As it happened the hike had gone exactly as she planned, although the critical test was yet to come. Leaving the minibus at the roadside they had climbed the slope of Merlin's Loaf, a massive outcrop jutting upwards into the valley. She had led them along a track that was popular with hikers, made distinct by them. A safe way that brought them to within a few paces of the cliff face. The track carried on, circling the top of the table to meet itself and descend. A path that was the way they had come but not the way they would leave.

Eileen took a flask of coffee from her rucksack and four paper cups that were jammed together. They had moved back to the path, a few paces from the cliff edge. She half-filled two of the cups and handed one to Fara. The girl walked away and sat down by Leem.

The second cup was given to Rees. "Don't act so tough," she told him, keeping her voice too low for the others to hear. "We are not down yet."

His response was a shift of gaze to the cliff edge. She saw his eyes widen. "My oh my, Miss Porter, you had me going there."

She smiled at him. His accent, a mix of West Indian and London cockney, sounded oddly musical, akin almost to Welsh.

He frowned at her. "Are you serious?" he asked, his voiced edged with disbelief.

"Deadly serious," she replied.

She beckoned Leem next and waited for him to reach her before pouring his coffee. Last of all she poured her own. The coffee was milky and sweet, loaded with sugar.

Fara raised her hand. "Miss Porter. You promised I'd get my ciggies back."

Eileen tossed the packet of cigarettes to the girl and watched her light one. Her bobbed hair was dyed a deep red. She was of mixed descent, part Asian, part Liverpool Irish, small and wiry, pretty in a provocative way.

The girl blew a cloud of smoke at Rees. He had carried his coffee to the flat rock. She seemed even tinier next to him, he was six feet tall and muscular. "Want a drag, tough boy?"

He waved away the smoke, ignoring the packet she offered.

Leem leaned past him, his hand outstretched, but Fara moved the packet beyond his reach. He pouted. "Aw, come on, Fara. Give me a puff."

"I asked Rees, not you."

"Why only him? What's wrong with me?"

"You slobber, that's why." She turned ack to Rees. "He reminds me of a drooly runt my bleeding dad put down."

Leem uttered a sob. "You scouse bitch!"

"Skank!" Farah responded.

Eileen was listening and watching. She emptied the grainy remains of her coffee. "All right. We have had our break. Time to start back."

Their sullen behaviour vanished in a flash, their faces alight with eagerness and enthusiasm.

It was the reaction Eileen expected, she had promised them a night out after the hike. It was a way of getting them on board without revealing any of the details or her motive. The promise had acted like a magical charm. Only Leem questioned her. "Why us, miss?"

"It wouldn't be right to tell you now."

Before leaving the minibus at the roadside she opened the rear door. There were four rucksacks, prepared and stowed by herself. They had no knowledge of what lay inside them.

"A change of gear, that kind of stuff," she explained and fastened one on each of them.

Now she emptied her own, item by item. "Climbing gear. I'll show you how all this works."

At length, when they were wearing the harness, the attachments, the hard-soled shoes, and were linked together by rope, Eileen attached a climbing rope to herself. She spoke to Rees. "I'll start down with Leem. Then Fara and you. Wait for my signal."

Rees grinned at Leem. "Wetting your pants, blood?"

Eileen gripped his arm and moved him to the cliff edge.

Leem swayed a little, his eyes pinned by the sheer drop to the valley that had opened-up beneath them. "Please, Miss Porter. I am feeling sort of dizzy."

Eileen's voice sharpened. "Then don't look down." She released her grip and turned to the others. "I know it's rather scary the first time. The trick is to keep your eyes on me. Where I place each foot, how I grip the rock. Understood?"

Without waiting for a reply, she started down.

Fara gave Leem a shove. "You next, slobber-mouth. Then me."

Leem followed Eileen, not daring to look beyond her. They reached a rocky outcrop. Eileen twitched the rope and waited to see Fara follow before continuing her descent. They proceeded in the same order and manner until, at length, they came together on a narrow ledge.

Leem kept his eyes on Eileen. "Are we there yet, Miss?"

"Nearly." Eileen had made the climb several times before, she knew every footfall and handhold of the way.

She started to edge along to the final point of descent several paces away where the ledge widened. Leem stayed close to her, stepping cautiously where she stepped.

Farah was following Rees. "Teacher's pet," she said to him, not loud enough for Eileen to hear.

Rees picked up a loose piece of rock and tossed it upwards. "Leem. Watch out!"

The chunk of rock hit the cliff face, bouncing close to him. He jerked away, losing his footing. "Miss Porter!"

Eileen turned her head and saw Leem pitch over the side. She braced herself, tried to hang on, stay on the ledge, but his weight dragged her with him. Dangling she managed to take a grip on the rock face with a climbing axe. She looked up.

Rees smiled down at her. "You and him hanging out together?"

He pulled back on the rope, and Eileen climbed to join him on the ledge. They hauled up Leem.

Eileen showed her annoyance. "That was stupid of you, Rees. It could have ended badly."

"Yeah, you are right, I *am* stupid. If I had a brain, I wouldn't have got caught by the cops, would I?"

She ignored him and turned to Leem. He was ashen-faced and shivering. "Come on. Not far to go now."

The boy shrank back, crouching. "No. Not yet." He shuddered. "I need a couple of minutes, Miss Porter."

The sky was darkening. "We are losing daylight." She looked at her wristwatch. "All right. Two minutes."

Rees frowned at Leem. "Man, you are gonna mess up our big night out."

"I don't care. I got the shakes." Leem held out a hand to Fara that trembled like a leaf. "Give me a ciggie, will you?"

"When we get down. I promise."

"Please. I must have a smoke."

"That won't help. What you need is a fix."

"You mean bitch."

"And you're nothing but a drag, slobber-mouth." The girl looked up at the others. "Why don't we just leave him here?"

Eileen checked her watch again. "Time to go."

Leem's voice strengthened a little. "No, wait. Please."

"Untie his rope, Rees," Eileen said. She turned to face Leem again. "Keep yourself warm. Don't fall asleep. We'll be back first thing in the morning."

Leem straightened up entirely. He held out a hand that had become as steady as a rock. "It's all right. I'm fine now."

Eileen looked hard at him before moving on with the descent. Leem followed her down.

***

Unseen by the four climbers two men in a black Range Rover were watching them. One, the owner of the car, was Ralph Smithson, principal officer of a Young Offenders Institute, a balding man of middle age, the second was a Californian, forty years old, who gave his name to the other as Jason Bligh. They had met for the first time at eleven o'clock that morning in the principal's office.

His arrival was expected by Ralph Smithson. A request had come from Los Angeles Prison Authority for a meeting where they could discuss and compare their methods of dealing with juvenile delinquents, and perhaps learn something from each other. Ralph Smithson took this as a compliment and agreed immediately. What surprised him was that the American wanted to speak to Eileen Porter, a recent addition to his staff.

They were sitting, facing each other across his desk. "Oh dear," he replied. "Miss Porter is out on an all-day hike. Will tomorrow morning suit you?"

"No, it won't. I have a flight to LA booked at midnight."

"How unfortunate." Smithson sighed. "Perhaps a phone conversation with her will do. I am sure you will be able to cover the ground adequately."

"Not at all, the discussion must be in person. And it will have to be today, I have a return flight booked." The American leaned forward in his chair. "Do you know where I can find her?"

"Of course." Smithson's voice became frosty. "I never allow young offenders under my supervision to leave the Institute without knowing where they are being taken."

"Certainly not," the American agreed. "A hike, you said. Is that far? Can I take a cab there?"

Smithson resisted the temptation to end the matter. Good manners must take precedence, he told himself, they demanded that he help the man. "It's a distance away, Mr Bligh," he said. "I'll drive you there myself if you want?"

"Gee, that sounds great." The American rose to his feet. "We can get to know each other much better on the way."

The Range Rover was in its customary place in the staff parking area. "Nice auto, Ralph," Jason said. They had exchanged first names on the way down from his office.

Smithson glanced at the dashboard clock before starting up the engine. "It's almost eleven thirty."

"When did Miss Porter set out?"

He glanced at the clock again. "An hour and a half ago. But we have plenty of time. She won't leave the site before dusk."

Reaching the main road, a dual carriageway, he kept the speed at a steady 70 mph. Overtaking a juggernaut truck, the needle crept to ninety.

The American turned to him after they were safely past the truck. "Why the rush?"

"A pub lunch, old chap. The local inn does a very good one. And we have time to kill."

"Hey, you've got it all worked out."

Smithson chuckled. "Hitting two birds with one stone, you could say."

"Tell me about the hike, how it fits into your programme," Jason asked him when they were nearly there, climbing a road on the hillside. Up till then the topic of juvenile delinquency had not been mentioned, their conversation had ranged over other matters.

Ralph Smithson paused before answering. He was not at all sure that the hike fitted his programme. The whole idea had come from the Porter woman. Avoiding the issue, he described the appeal of Merlin's Loaf to hikers, to naturalists, to birdwatchers such as himself. "The area is as close to untouched by human hand as you can find in these parts."

"Is that so? You should come to the States then. Plenty of wide, open space over there."

They passed the minibus parked on the roadside soon after, a reminder to Ralph Smithson that he still had no idea why the American wanted to meet Eileen Porter.

All at once he understood why he had decided to make the journey with him. The reason was not good manners or his liking for a pub meal. It was because asking the man directly why he wanted to meet the Porter woman was beneath his dignity. Instead, he had driven him here to learn his purpose first-hand.

About a mile beyond the minibus, the car took a turning to the right. The turning, barely wider than a lane, carried no name and no destination. It wound downhill through trees and shrubs, a forested area colourful in early Spring.

The slope, steep at first, flattened, the muddy lane became a road, they had reached the floor of the valley.

Smithson eased his grip on the steering wheel. "Almost there," he said and followed the road to where it ended, at the inn.

The *Merlin Arms*, a grey, gaunt building, seemed as old and as weather-beaten as the mountain and cliffs on either side. There was an extensive parking area outside the entrance. It was almost empty, but Ralph Smithson pulled up on the far edge, facing a cliff that jutted out a distance away. He shivered when they climbed out of the car, the air had become noticeably colder, close to freezing.

The lunch menu was chalked up on a board outside: *Crème de tomate, Truite aux amandes.* "Tomato soup followed by freshly caught river trout roasted with almonds," Ralph Smithson explained. "We can order at the bar."

Inside, the inn felt warm and cosy.

"Just a sandwich for me, pal," Jason said when they reached the bar.

Smithson felt disappointed. "What is it, jet lag?"

"I guess so."

"A drink, then. What are you having?"

"Do they serve coffee here?"

The barman answered. "Black or white, sir?"

"Black, for me."

Ralph Smithson asked for two cheddar cheese sandwiches and two black coffees. It wouldn't do to eat a cooked meal on his own. And he was overweight anyway.

The barman placed two paper bags and two paper cups of coffee on the counter. Jason picked up a coffee and a paper bag. "How about we eat outside? A breath of fresh air will do us good."

Ralph Smithson paid the barman, took hold of the other paper bag and coffee cup and followed the American out of the *Merlin Arms.* Once again, a shiver ran through him. A wintry day in March, grey and overcast, with hardly a hint of Spring. He made straight for the Range Rover parked on the gravelled area, a spot reserved for visitors to the valley. He climbed in, closing the door. From there he had an unimpeded view of the cliff through the windscreen.

Opening the paper bag, he found a sliced half loaf of French bread bulging with cheese, Branston pickle, raw onion, tomato, cucumber, and lettuce. It tasted delicious, more like a ploughman's lunch than a cheese sandwich.

***

Jason Bligh ate outside. After finishing the pub lunch, he took care to deposit the debris of the meal - the bag, the paper napkin, the plastic coffee cup - in a rubbish container nearby. His eyes had been fixed while eating on the cliff that rose to maybe fifteen hundred feet above the valley. He understood why the local people named the cliff Merlin's Loaf. The part that faced him was sheer rock, as if the end of the outcrop had been sliced off by King Arthur's sword.

He climbed into the front passenger seat of the Range Rover. "What now, Ralph?" he asked.

Ralph Smithson sighed. "Very little, I'm afraid. We wait here."

"For what?"

"Until we catch sight of them. The path runs along the top of the cliff."

"And then what?"

"We drive to the minibus."

"Where we wait again?"

"That is correct."

"How long before dusk."

"I'm not sure." Smithson looked at the dashboard clock. The time showed 14:05. "A little after two o'clock. It starts to get dark around four."

Jason used a handkerchief to wipe sweat from his brow. The engine was running, the heater on. "Kind of hot in here, don't you think?"

"Let me see." Smithson checked the heater gauge. "It's on ambient."

Jason pocketed the handkerchief. "Do you mind if I step outside again? I can keep watch from there."

"Not a bit." Smithson leaned across and brought a pair of binoculars from the glove box. "You will see better with these. I use them for birdwatching."

Jason leaned back into the car for his raincoat, leaving the door open until he had the coat buttoned with the collar turned up. He kept close to the car, using it as a shield against the wind, lifting his gaze to the cliff-top from time to time. A while went by before a glance revealed three climbers looking out at the valley.

Smithson's binoculars were hanging around his neck. He raised the eyeglasses and tracked up the cliff face to the three figures, focussing first on the woman. She was tall, athletic looking, her fair hair gathered into a ponytail. His focus moved on to the two teenagers. One was dark-skinned, tall and broad-shouldered, the other a girl, small with short red hair. All three wore jeans and leather jackets.

He tapped on the driver window. Smithson had stayed behind the wheel throughout. The window lowered. He offered the binoculars. "Take a look. There, at the top of the cliff."

Smithson ignored the eyeglasses. "Whoever you saw has gone."

The climbers had moved out of sight. Jason described the woman. "A good-looking blonde."

"That is Miss Porter, all ri1ght," Smithson muttered.

"I get the feeling she intends to climb down."

Smithson snorted. "Certainly not. It's much too risky," he said and closed the window of the Range Rover.

Jason stayed outside with the binoculars, leaning back against the car. After a while, the climbers reappeared, all four of them this time. They were wearing climbing gear. He tapped on the driver's window again and pointed upwards.

Smithson came out muffled in his overcoat and scarf.

Jason put the binoculars to his eyes again. "You are right, Ralph. Climbing down that cliff-face is no cakewalk."

Smithson held out his hand. "May I?"

Jason gave him the eyeglasses and watched him angle them shakily up the cliff to the top. "Good heavens! It's bloody dangerous."

"Isn't putting them in danger the whole idea of this jaunt?"

"Not at all." Smithson lowered the binoculars. "There could be a serious accident."

"I guess Miss Porter knows what she is about."

"That's all very well, Mr Bligh. But the three delinquents with her happen to be *my* responsibility."

Jason's gaze returned to the clifftop. Two of the figures were starting down. "You had better start praying then, Mr Smithson. They are on their way."

"Oh dear," Smithson said, his voice shaky.

Jason took the eyeglasses from him. "It's okay. Go back inside, I'll keep watch."

Jason was outside the car watching when the quartet reached the foot of the cliff.

He had tracked their descent throughout. Daylight was fading into dusk but looking at them through the binoculars they seemed elated, they were embracing each other.

Smithson was hunched over the steering wheel. Jason climbed into the passenger seat beside him. "They are down. You can uncross your fingers."

Smithson raised his head. "I am perfectly relaxed, old chap."

He offered the binoculars. "Do you want to take a look?"

Smithson released the handbrake. "No, I will take your word for it."

Jason returned the eyeglasses to the glove box. "Quite a gal, your Miss Porter."

The vehicle jerked forward. "That is a matter of opinion, Mr Bligh."

***

Eileen watched the teenagers hug each other. She wanted to join in, kiss them, tell them how proud she was, but that moment would come on the night out when the hike was done.

The descent had brought them to the valley at the foot of Merlin's Loaf, a stretch of two miles roughly from where they had left the minibus about four and a half hours ago. She waited for them to calm down. "All done with that?" They nodded as if embarrassed. "Very well then. Let's go."

The ground was uneven and tiring to clamber over, a scree of fallen fragments, tocks and boulders, some of them quite large. The teenagers hardly spoke a word to each other on the trudge. An unnatural silence that troubled Eileen and made her begin to wonder whether the hike had been a mistake, a waste of effort and time.

She led the way until the teenagers caught sight of the minibus parked as they had left it in a layby on the roadside. They burst ahead of her, joyfully. Fara and Leem were arm-in-arm, Rees in the lead backing away from them in a boxing stance, jabbing both fists, left, left, right.

All at once Eileen felt light as air, her doubts gone. She approached the minibus, ignition key in hand. Fatigue had wearied the teenagers, kept them silent on the trudge. Now they were waiting for her eagerly, a united band. The hike was a success, something to celebrate.

A black Land Rover screeched to a halt in front of her, a car that she recognised, and for an instant she thought that perhaps the principal of the Institute had come to congratulate her. Any such hope ended when she saw him get out of the car. His face was set in stone, his posture aggressive.

He strode towards her. "I saw what happened up there. Totally unprofessional."

"Spying on me, Ralph?" she asked.

"You endangered young lives. Recklessly, in my opinion."

She frowned. "There has to be some risk in a project such as this, otherwise where is the challenge? And they have come through all the better for it."

"I doubt that. As of now, the project is cancelled."

She glanced at the man who was with him in the car. He had stepped out and was listening. "Shouldn't we be discussing the matter in private?"

"Mr Bligh is a colleague from California, here to learn our methods. I imagine he is far from impressed with what he has seen."

Despite herself, she looked at the American, waiting for him to reply. He gave her a shrug, as if his opinion hardly mattered.

"Are you his bodyguard, bro?" Rees asked him.

Smithson answered. "That's enough from you, boy." It was the principal's usual response to even the mildest hint of rebellion. He turned his attention back to her. "I want them back this evening."

She shook her head. "Tomorrow, Ralph. I promised them a night out. And they are going to have one."

The teenagers whooped.

Ralph Smithson glared at her. "Very well." He turned away. "I shall expect you in my office at ten sharp tomorrow morning."

"There is no need for that. You will get my letter of resignation."

"As you wish, Miss Porter," he said and climbed back into his car.

His colleague from California, Mr Bligh, lingered for a moment, long enough to give her another shrug, this time a sympathetic one. He was tall, well-built, with an easy-going manner.

"It isn't fair, Miss Porter," Fara said when they were gone.

She sighed. "Perhaps Mr Smithson is right. That was a hairy moment we had up there."

Leem bowed his head. "I am sorry about that, Miss."

"Don't be. You came good, and I am proud of you. *All* of you."

"Shit, that don't count for nothing with him," Rees said. "The man is a total arsehole."

"Right on." She unlocked the minibus doors. "The hell with it. Let's have that night out."

***

For their night together Eileen had chosen a hotel in a small town about twenty miles beyond the turn-off that had taken them to Merlin's Loaf. An establishment that was old-fashioned in a genteel way according to the hotel guide handbook, a description confirmed by the manager on the phone.

She had taken three rooms and booked dinner for four. In a sneaky fashion, it was a chance to see how well they had bonded. Three teenagers, oddly matched, with nothing in common, in a place that was totally alien to their experience. A true test of her project.

She pulled up outside the hotel entrance, it had started to rain and there was no place nearby to park the minibus. She spoke to Rees because he was the oldest of the trio. "I'm letting you out here. Everything is arranged. You and Leem share a room, Fara gets a room to herself."

They clambered out, taking their backpacks with them. "Do you want me to bring your one, Miss?" Fara asked.

"No. I can manage." Everything that she needed was in her briefcase.

Searching for a space large enough for the minibus took Eileen a while, the *Westward Inn* lay at the centre of the town, a mostly no-parking zone. The spot she found at last was several side streets away from the hotel. Arriving back with her briefcase, she was glad there was no sign of the teenagers waiting anxiously for her. She was soaked, her hair a mess, the rain had become a downpour. And in any case, there was a more pressing matter on her mind, the letter of resignation.

A burly man wearing a bowtie eyed her. He was standing arms folded behind the reception desk, evidently the hotel manager. The reception clerk next to him was young, sandy-haired, hardly older than the teenagers. "Eileen Porter," she told him. "I have a room booked."

He went over to the board of hooks at the rear and picked out one of the door-keys.

"What time is dinner," she asked.

"Not for a while yet. The dining room opens at eight, closes at ten."

He gave her the key. It was old and heavy, stamped with a number. "Room eighteen," she said. "Which floor?"

"The third. We have a lift. Or there is a staircase if you prefer."

She used the lift, the only item in sight that seemed less than a hundred years old.

Opening the door marked '18', she saw a room in which the carpet, the curtains, the wallpaper, the bedspread, were a uniform match in dull brown, and the furniture – a double bed, a wardrobe, bedside table, a bureau desk, an armchair - a match in darker brown.

The room was over-heated and had a musty smell as if unused and un-aired for some time. She opened a window. Below, an expanse of cobblestones glistening in the rain reached a line of shops on the far side. The hotel looked out onto the town's market square.

A peep into the bathroom revealed a huge bathtub with a shower head on the wall above the taps. A sign read *'Kindly close the shower curtain when in use'*.

A shiver ran through her. A shiver caused by nothing more than the coldness brought on by the wet clothes on her, she told herself. She stripped them off in the bathroom, leaving only her panties on, and squeezed as much wetness from them as she could over the basin before draping the still-damp t-shirt, jeans, and socks on the hot towel rail. They would be dry after a long bath.

The bathtub was slowly filling. She had turned the tap marked 'H' for Hot full on but the water that came out was scarcely more than a dribble. Waiting there, another shiver ran through her. It prompted her to leave the bathroom, the tap still running.

She sat down at the small bureau desk and opened the briefcase. Her letter to Ralph Smithson was brief, written with a fountain pen.

Ralph,

Today you made perfectly clear to me (and to others) that you do not approve of my methods. Under the circumstances I see no purpose in continuing at the Institute. Please accept this as a letter of resignation.

Eileen Porter.

She folded the sheet into an envelope. The future had become uncertain. What next, she wondered.

Aged thirty-seven years, and adventurous by nature, Eileen Porter had faced pivotal moments often before in her life. In 'live or die' situations, her reaction was always spontaneous, there was no time for leisurely reflection. In other less threatening moments, such as now, her thoughts became clouded and confused. As ever her response was to shift her energy to hard physical activity. A work-out that would clear her mind.

She reached into the briefcase for the leotard, one designed for dancers. It was always there along with the fountain pen. All three, the tortoise-shell pen, the black leotard, the tan leather briefcase, were birthday presents from her brother. If he were still alive, he would be forty this summer.

She returned to the bathroom wearing the leotard. The air inside was hot and steamy, the tub full to the brim. Leaving the door open behind her, she shut off the hot water tap and wiped the mirrored wall above the bath clear of moisture, using a hand towel. Watching herself, she repeated her morning routine, fifteen minutes of ballet muscle stretching exercises, though now they were practised with maximum vigour. Tall, deep-chested, broad-shouldered in appearance, her figure seemed to belong to the polar opposite of a half-starved ballerina. She smiled. Not the sort of woman a dancing partner would care to whirl around the stage.

After ten minutes of the routine, she was sweating profusely, but her doubts had gone. Uncommanded, her subconscious mind had refocused and identified the dilemma. The letter left propped against her brief case would decide her destiny: a psychotherapist without a job.

She sat down at the bureau desk, the letter in her hand, and reached for the waste basket beneath. Next morning, she would apologise to Ralph Smithson in his office. A knock on the door made her pause.

Another knock. "Hey, Miss Porter? Are you there?" The voice belonged to an American.

Before answering she tore the letter in two and dropped the pieces into the basket. "Who is it?"

"Jason Bligh. The guy who watched you come down that cliff." For some unknown reason, her heart thumped.

Her heart raced more when she saw him standing in the doorway. His eyes surveyed her. They were blue flecked with gold like her brother's.

"Are you planning on a cross country run or a raiding party?" he asked.

She sighed. "At the moment it seems more like a wake to me."

"I guess you didn't tell the rest of the bunch. Right now, they are in the bar blowing up a storm."

"Thanks for telling me." She turned back to the desk.

"You don't seem concerned."

"I'm not. It's part of their rehabilitation process."

He closed the door and came over to her. "Mind if I stick around, Miss Porter? I might learn something."

"Not a bit, Mr Bligh. But I'll be awhile, and I doubt whether this hotel does room service."

Her stay in the bathroom lasted less than twenty minutes. She drained the bathtub, the water had gone cold, and took a shower. She came out dressed, her clothes had dried on the towel rail. He was sitting at the bureau desk in the easy chair, his eyes closed. She wondered whether he had pieced the letter together. In a way, she hoped that he had.

He opened his eyes. "That was quick. I mean, women generally take much longer in the bathroom."

She raised an eyebrow. "You are married, aren't you?"

"Some of the time." He met her gaze. "Does that bother you?"

"Why would it?" All at once his self-assurance became a challenge. "What the hell are you doing here in the hotel anyway?"

"I thought I might learn something."

"And have you?"

"Yeah. The barman told me that well brought up English girls drink gin and tonic before dinner."

She hadn't noticed, there were two drinks on the bureau desk. He handed a glass to her. They had moved onto the bed. She swallowed a mouthful and felt the warm glow of whisky, not the icy coldness of gin. "Scotch?"

"Bourbon." He put his hand on her thigh. "Whisky seems to suit you better."

Does he think I am not well brought up? she wondered.

His hand moved up and unzipped her jeans. She felt his fingers glide to where she was still damp from the shower. Her response was instinctive. She turned her back to him and lay flat on the bed.

***

Eileen followed him down a narrow stairway, a continuation of the main staircase of the hotel. It led to the basement. A blast of sound greeted them when he opened the door. Leem was playing electric guitar, accompanied by the barman on bongos, and with Fara dancing on the bar-top urged on by Rees.

Jason gripped her hand. "Wait." They stayed by the door, unnoticed.

The hotel manager strode past them. "You! Stop that bloody racket."

The man behind the bar froze. Eileen remembered him, the reception clerk who had given her the room-key.

"You idiot," the manager said. "Turn off your blasted guitar."

The young barman zeroed the volume control of the amplifier. Leem carried on playing acoustically, his fingers moving like a spider along the keyboard.

"That ain't polite, rude boy." Rees leaned over the bar to the amplifier and turned the volume control upward again.

The noise was louder than before. The manager pulled out the wall-plug. "I want you lot out of here."

Leem stopped fingering the guitar. "Why, mister? We ain't doing no harm."

The manager took hold of Leem. "You are leaving because I say so."

Rees moved aggressively towards the manager.

Eileen stepped between them, holding the teenager off. "I will deal with the situation, Rees." She turned to the manager. "There is no need to be heavy-handed. He is only a boy."

"A boy?" The manager released Leem. "Very well, have it your way." He glared at the barman. "Call the police."

"Boss, they were only drinking cokes, having a little fun."

"You heard me. Now do as I say."

The barman threw a sorrowful glance at Leem before picking up the phone.

Jason caught the manager's eye. "Listen, why bother with the cops? It's over, they are done."

The barman hesitated. The manager grabbed the phone from him.

"Hold it, pal." Jason reached into his pocket and brought out a wallet. "Maybe this will help change your mind." He offered some banknotes. "To cover any damage caused. Or possible loss of trade."

The manager put down the receiver. "All right. That sounds fair." He folded the banknotes into the bar till. "But I want these hooligans out of here. Out of my hotel."

Jason looked at Eileen.

Eileen nodded and turned to the others. "All of you, get your stuff and wait for me outside." She remembered her briefcase and gave key number eighteen to Fara. "Collect my briefcase, would you? I left it on the desk."

Jason walked with her to the minibus. The rain had stopped. "How much did you give him?" she asked.

"The ass-hole manager? No idea. Does it matter?"

"Yes, you saved the day. How can I repay you?"

"I'll give that some thought."

His reply suggested his intention was to stay with them on the ride back to the institute. She checked the time on her wristwatch. Eight-thirty, they should arrive there by ten unless they stopped to eat on the way.

Neither of them said a word returning in the mini-bus to the hotel. The youngsters were waiting for them on the pavement outside. Fara handed over the briefcase when they climbed in. "I didn't open it, Miss."

"Certainly not," she said, knowing very well that the girl had looked inside and most likely tried on the leotard. A sigh escaped her lips. An outing in which no one had been entirely honest. Least of all, perhaps, herself.

She moved off, the vehicle bumping over the cobblestones. Jason gave a yawn he was sitting with her upfront. She glanced at him. His eyes were shut.

The next time she heard hm speak they were travelling over a stretch of motorway. "Well, what do you know? The hell-raisers have fallen asleep."

She looked at them over her shoulder. All three were sprawled out, their eyes closed, on seats at the back. A peaceful feeling settled on her. "Thanks for helping them avoid the police."

He frowned. "Avoid the cops? That makes me seem like an accomplice."

She explained. "They are youngsters. Kids who have never had a decent chance in life."

"Okay, you gave them a fair crack at one. A shame they screwed up."

She looked at him. "No, you are wrong. *I* blew it, not them." Her gaze stayed fixed on him an instant longer. "Who *are* you, anyway, Mr Bligh?"

"A fan of yours, Miss Porter."

"Stop putting me on." She laughed wryly. "You should know by now, I'm not that good in bed."

"I disagree, but anyhow that's not the reason I came. How about this." He opened his notebook and read aloud. "'The establishment of team spirit is a key factor in the rehabilitation of young offenders...'"

"All right. You have read my book." Her grunt was scornful. "But that was before learning that my methods don't work."

"Not with Ralph Smithson calling the shots. With me it would be a whole lot different ball game."

She allowed herself a half-smile. "Are you offering me a job?"

"I guess you need one, don't you?"

"Look, I lost my temper with him, that's all. An abject apology should do the trick." She gave a sigh. "You are right, though. Ralph Smithson is a pain in the arse. However, I can't simply run out on the kids, can I?"

"You won't have to. Your three. And my three." Jason clasped his hands together, fingers interlocked. "A combined op."

"A great idea." She sighed. "Except you'll never get Ralph to buy it."

"Honey, he already has."

She looked at the American wide-eyed.

Rees leaned forward and exchanged high-fives with him. "Right on!" He had been awake and listening throughout.

***

"We should talk," he said after she dropped the three youngsters at the Institute. "Get to know each other better."

"You must be hungry." She looked at her wristwatch. The dial showed a little after nine-thirty, and they had driven all the way without stopping. "Do you have time for a meal?"

"Sure."

She drove the minibus to her hotel, which lay on the entry road of the town about three to four miles from the Institute, a distance that she generally cycled. Her accommodation was paid for by them, though not her meals. One of a chain of franchises, streamlined and functional, the hotel was a stark contrast to the genteel one she had chosen for the night out.

The restaurant served them grilled steak and chips and a decent bottle of burgundy. Mostly they talked shop.

"We have problems handling young offenders in LA," Jason admitted. "In the worst districts, mostly with street gangs."

"Do you think my method might work with them?"

"Street gangs? Yes, I do. That's why I came over."

"Good heavens," she gasped, covering her face with her hands.

"Did I say something wrong?"

She shook her head.

"What, then?" he asked.

She uncovered her face and tried to smile. "Street gangs made me change my job."

"How come?"

She hated talking about her past, it brought a sense of shame. "Not now. Some other time, perhaps."

"Yeah. I feel the same way as you." He squeezed her hand. "It's the future that matters."

His touch thrilled her in a way that surprised her. Their lovemaking a few hours ago at the *Westward Inn* had been brief, perfunctory. Afterwards each of them behaved as though their intimate encounter had never occurred.

It was around eleven when they finished their meal. "What time is your flight?" she asked.

"Not for a while yet."

A sense that the night was unfinished made her say, "I'll show you my room, if you like."

The bar was still open. He bought a bottle of scotch, a single malt. They took the lift to the top floor. The room was small, uncluttered, with a view from the window of farmland and, beyond, the far-off glow of the town.

He half-filled two glasses. She took a large swallow.

He eyed her. "I get the impression you are ex-military."

"Me?" She laughed. "What makes you think that?"

"It takes a vet to recognise a vet." His eyes stayed on her. "Army?"

On this occasion, she dropped her guard. "No, the air force, I joined at eighteen."

"Air crew?"

"Yes, I trained as a pilot." Once started she carried on, he was a good listener. "I flew just about everything they had to offer, from fighter jets to helicopters."

"I guess you must have fought in Iraq?"

"Yes." She sighed. A vision of a road came into her mind. A dusty treeless road, a column of fleeing soldiers. The twin rocket missiles she launched cut down swathes of them.

"Where did you operate?"

"I don't remember." She blinked. "Eventually they sent me to the city of Baghdad. I spoke Arabic, you see, my father was Army, stationed in Aden." She blinked again. "It was a pivotal moment in my life."

"In what way?"

"They had me deal with young people. A woman's touch, I suppose. I saw that the street gangs gave kids a common purpose. Loyalty to each other. I got to know them. I felt responsible."

He grunted. "Yeah, it's the same in Los Angeles."

"Is that where you live?"

"Mostly."

She took another swallow, the last of the whisky, and kissed him on the cheek. There were no chairs, they were sitting together on her bed. "You remind me of someone."

"Who might that be?"

An image of her brother flashed into her mind. She laid down her glass and kissed him hard on the lips, her hand on his crotch. She felt him harden.

He reached for the zip of her denim jeans.

"No, not you this time," she said. "Let me."

She pushed him back on the bed and unbuckled his belt. "Put your hands behind your head."

He obeyed her.

She pulled his trousers down below his knees and sat astride him. He was helpless, the way she wanted.

THREE: EXPEDITION ANONYMOUS

The noise of the aircraft engines woke Eileen, a change of tone that denoted the jetliner was coming-in to land. She was in an aisle seat but a tilt of the wings
gave her a view through the porthole of the lit-up runway of an airport at night that she knew must be LA International. A light was flashing above her, *Fasten Seatbelts.* Leaning forward, a glance at the teenagers confirmed that all three had belted up.

The digital watch she wore showed 11:15 am, it was still registering Greenwich Mean Time not Pacific Standard Time. Her heart raced, how quickly everything had happened! The time was a reminder that the call from Jason Bligh had come through on her mobile less than twenty-four hours ago. She was supervising a football game in a caged area used for that purpose at the Youth Offenders Institute.

"Good news," he said. "Your side of the op starts out tonight from Heathrow." He gave her the departure time of the flight, the eta at LA Airport.

She hid her excitement. "What happens when we get there, Jason?"

His tone became brisk. You meet up with my three young offenders."

"Great. But where are we heading next?" Quite evidently the city of Los Angeles was not the destination of the hike.

"Listen," he replied. "You will be given a file at the airport on arrival. It contains everything you need to know."

She gave a snort. "Entitled 'Expedition Anonymous', I suppose."

"All right, I can tell you this much. A plane will bring all of you to me here in Heronimo County."

"Heronimo? Where on earth is that?"

"You will find it on the map in the file," he said, and ended the call.

Everything had gone as he promised. A limousine, a Jaguar, arrived at the institute at three o'clock, drove them to Heathrow Airport, the jetliner took off on time at midnight, and now almost twelve hours later she was looking down at an LAX runway.

Rees opened the storage cabinet and handed out their luggage, the aircraft had landed smoothly and taxied to a halt. He was closest in the seat by the window. She had issued each of them and herself with a military style duffel bag. Along with the rest of the passengers they entered an attached corridor that led directly into the terminal building.

A dark-haired smartly dressed woman was waiting for them at Passport Control. "Miss Porter?"

She nodded, and they followed the woman to a small private lounge. The décor was discreet, the seating comfortable, the floor thickly carpeted, clearly a refuge for VIPs. A waiter served them with breakfast, they were alone there. The youngsters sat huddled together on a huge sofa, talking in whispers. She left them and took a seat by a smoked-glass window that looked out onto the airport.

Her thoughts turned to Jason Bligh. The call on her mobile was the first that she had heard from him since the night spent together in her hotel room.

Was she in love with the American? she wondered.

Certainly not, she decided, they were much too alike, too self-possessed. It was the expedition into the unknown which excited her, not him.

Eileen Porter laid down the upmarket property magazine held in her hand. The sky had paled into morning and through the window she saw that a small bus had pulled up outside on the tarmac. Moments later she heard her name called. "Miss Porter."

The voice belonged to the smartly dressed woman. She was standing behind her holding a large manilla envelope.

"Is that for me?" she asked.

The woman nodded and gave her the envelope.

It was sealed and felt thin and light. "Is the file inside?"

"I have no idea, Miss Porter. It's time for you to leave. The driver is waiting."

The teenagers were on their feet, the duffel bags over their shoulders, eager to be on their way. The woman led them out through a side door to the waiting bus. Though still early morning, the air was warm and scented.

They climbed in. The interior was bare, with overhead hanging leather straps, the seats made of unpadded wood, a vehicle designed to carry airport work people not flight passengers like themselves.

Eileen was the last to enter. The driver, a burly man, closed the folding door behind her.

The bus conveyed them through the holding area of the airport, passing between the humped shapes of huge airliners shrouded in early morning mist, to a much smaller aircraft, an aeroplane with twin piston engines tucked away in a secluded section. A pilot was in the cockpit checking the controls.

There was seating for sixteen passengers, four rows of two on either side of the aisle. Eileen chose a seat opposite the boarding entry door, giving her sight of the holding area, the way they had come, the likely route of Jason's party. She unsealed the envelope, taking care not to tear the paper. A folder made of yellow cardboard lay inside. Opening the flap revealed a personnel list, three typewritten sheets stapled together, a map, and three name tags.

The typewritten sheets dealt with Jason Bligh's three young offenders. She decided to meet them face-to-face, to gain a first impression of them, before learning about their police records and misdemeanours.

The personnel list named herself and Jason as *Guides*, and two others described as *Guards*.

The name tags were the first names of Rees, Fara and Leem. They were sitting apart from each other. She watched them pin the tags on their t-shirts. "It feels like I'm for sale," Fara said.

Eileen returned to her seat. A glance behind her revealed Fara taking out a cigarette. She pointed at one of the *No Smoking* signs in the seating area. The girl scowled and put the cigarette back in the packet.

Sitting there, Eileen heard the portside propellor whirr into motion. The pilot was checking the engines. She had flown military transport aircraftpowered by piston engines, but never a civilian passenger version. Curiosity made her go up front.

The pilot looked up when she entered the cockpit. "I am Eileen Porter."

"Yeah, they told me." He scowledat her. "Listen, up here is for pilots not passengers."

"That all right, I used to be one. Military."

"Heck, no one told me that." His scowl became a smile. "Bill Perkin. Welcome on board."

She sat in the co-pilot seat and examined the controls. "It's a while since I flew a piston engine plane."

"I guess you're wondering why you're in one?"

"Yes, I am."

He grunted. "Heronimo airfield. No bigger than a postage stamp, so I'm told. Too tight to land a jet. Which is why we are using this baby."

"It's the approach that counts," she said. "Do you want a second pair of eyes up here?"

"Yeah. I could use your help."

The deep-throated rumble of an approaching vehicle brought her back to the boarding doorway. A heavily built truck was approaching across the tarmac. She watched it reverse and pull up about twenty metres away. Armour-plated, with a massive steel rear door, the vehicle seemed to be as safe a way of transporting valuable cargo as she could imagine.

The rear door swung inwards, and she saw a man carrying a brief case descend the three steps down to the tarmac. He wore a dark grey uniform and a cap marked *Prison Guard*. He looked up and came towards her. She knew his name, it was typed on the personnel list in the cardboard folder, *Dan Glasson*.

***

A young girl was next down the steps of the armoured truck. At the bottom, legs apart, her straight blonde hair hanging freely to her waist, she stretched upwards, as if reaching for the sky. Statuesque, barely sixteen years old, she had the form of a grown woman.

"What's the matter, Karin?" A second teenager was coming down the steps. Small in stature with shoulder length black hair, a Spanish guitar strapped across his back, like her he looked older than his years. "Your pussy itch, *chica*?"

"Is that a turn-on for you, shorty? Talking dirty?" She closed her eyes and breathed in through her nose. "We are in L.A., little man. I'd know the smell anywhere."

"*Si*, it stinks real good." He sniffed. "*Gasolina*." A shrug. "Do you think they put us in the movies here?"

She sighed. "Not unless you grow a whole lot taller and prettier, Raul." They had never met before, but she knew his name from the tag pinned to his jacket.

Grant Redd appeared in the doorway of the truck. A red-faced beefy man armed with a rifle, he reached in for the third teenager. The boy was handcuffed, hands behind his back. The prison guard hauled him out on to the steps.

Eileen met Dan Glasson before he reached the plane. Her manner was aggressive. She had seen the other prison guard shove the teenager from the truck, prod him with a rifle, "Whose idea were the handcuffs?"

Dan Glasson peered at her through his spectacles. "I take it you are Eileen Porter?"

"That is correct. Now answer me. Whose idea were the handcuffs and the gun?"

"Mr Bligh's, I guess. This one is dangerous, Miss Porter." Dan Glasson opened his briefcase and took out a copy of the three typed sheets. "Take a look at his make."

"On my hikes we all start out clean." By then the others had reached them, close enough for her to read the name tag on the handcuffed teenager: *Jon*. She turned to the armed guard. "Take the handcuffs off him, Mr Redd."

He grinned at her. "I don't have the key, lady."

Dan Glasson sighed. "It's okay, Grant. Do as the lady says."

Eileen watched the armed guard free the teenager before turning away to the airplane.

Raul and Karin climbed in after her.

Redd shoved Jon forward. "Move yourself, asshole." The teenager stumbled. Using the butt of his rifle Redd gave another shove. Jon faced up to him, fists bunched.

Dan Glasson moved between them. "Cut it out, Grant." He turned to Jon. "Use your head, boy."

The teenager got into the plane, hauling himself up. He joined the other two, standing with Eileen Porter in the seating aisle. Behind him the two guards closed and barred the door.

Eileen spread her arms. "How much do you know about all this?"

Raul grunted. "They don't say nothing. Are you gonna tell us we invited to an orgy?"

"Sorry to disappoint you, Raul."

"Something you ought to know," Karin said. "Talking dirty turns him on."

"Thanks for the information, Karin. Jon, do you have anything to say?"

"Yeah. Who are you?"

"My name is Eileen Porter. Your guide." The plane trembled. The pilot had started up the twin piston engines. "We will all get to know more about this later when we land." She spread her arms again. "You may sit wherever you please."

The British teenagers, who had picked seats separate from each other, were eying them. Jon took a seat at the rear, Karin huddled next to him, Raul sat close by.

The pilot's intercom crackled. "Fasten up back there."

Eileen checked their seatbelts one by one, starting with her own party. They were all fastened, except Karin's. The girl was panting, her face drained of colour. Eileen clicked the seatbelt shut. "Your first time, Karin? Have you never flown before?"

"No." The girl shuddered. "Boy, do I need a smoke."

Eileen straightened up. All eyes were on her. "Listen, does anyone have a cigarette?" Nobody responded. "How about you, Fara?"

The girl pointed at the *No Smoking* sign. "Can't the silly cow read?"

Eileen returned to her seat at the front, opposite the boarding door.

The airplane began to move, taxiing into position. All at once Karin released the seatbelt and made a bolt along the aisle for the exit.

Rees reached out and grabbed her. She struggled, but he pulled her onto his lap. "Give up, girl. This here bus ain't stopping for nobody."

Eileen smiled. In a sense one of her offenders had bonded with a newcomer. It was an encouraging sign.

The airplane gathered speed and lifted off. A few seconds later an unbroken blue sky showed through the portholes. The airplane banked towards the sun, low on the horizon. The plane was heading east. The pilot's voice came through on the intercom. "It's okay to move around now."

Rees let go of Karin. She staggered back to her seat.

Eileen freed her seatbelt and opened the flimsy cardboard file. She brought out the map and laid it out on her lap fold by fold. The map was detailed and multi-coloured, from pale yellow to dark blue, reflecting the land's height above sea-level. She ran her finger from the city of Los Angeles on the left to the town of Heronimo on the right. Using the scale at the top, she estimated the distance to go was about eight hundred miles. The route crossed three states, California, Arizona and New Mexico.

She unfolded the map fully. A highway ran to Heronimo, and beyond to San Petro on the Mexican border, but he area between the two towns was undefined, a blank white, as if the detail had been wiped away by a nuclear catastrophe.

Eileen moved onto the typewritten pages. The first page dealt with the two prison guards. Dan Glasson, aged forty-five, had worked as a prisoner officer for more than twenty years. His record was excellent, not a single blemish. Grant Redd, aged twenty-seven a trainee orderly, was a recent addition to the prison staff. An ex-Marine who had been dismissed from the Corps for insubordination a few months earlier.

She read the resumes of the three teenagers in the order that she had seen them, eager to know how closely they coincided with her first impressions.

Karen, aged sixteen, a San Franciscan, was guilty of a multitude of minor misdemeanours that began when she was hardly more than a child. They included petty theft, possession of narcotic drugs, soliciting.

Raul, aged seventeen, a native of Brooklyn, was a compulsive car thief. A dare-devil driver employed by thieves to drive the getaway car he had carried on driving the stolen Porsche from New York to Los Angeles. The LAPD arrested him for grand auto theft.

The paragraph on Jon was more like a footnote than a resume. Aged seventeen, he was described as a vagrant, violent, a knife-carrier, extremely dangerous. Unlike the reports on Karin and Raul, there was no police record or court appearance listed.

Eileen sighed. Jason Bligh's choice of offenders was by far harder-edged than her own. Will they mix? Would they share a common purpose? She turned to look at them behind her. Only Leem had moved, he was sitting nearer to Raul watching him pick out chords on his guitar. Her watch showed almost nine o'clock. They had been airborne about twenty-five minutes.

***

Music awoke Eileen. Turning her head, she saw that Leem had moved alongside Raul and was expertly fingering runs and chords on his Spanish guitar. Her watch had stopped, and she had no sense of time. The sun through a portside window opposite caught her eye. It showed much higher than before, the day had reached close to noon. More than two hours had passed.

They were flying above a rock desert, following the long straight ribbon of a highway. Looking through the window next to her, the faint outline of a mountainous range appeared in the distance.

A while passed, the airplane steadily losing height and speed. The wing tilted and she could see a side road branching off the highway two or three miles ahead. It led to a small township which she guessed must be Heronimo.

The pilot's voice came through on the intercom. "Fasten seatbelts. We'll be touching down soon."

She made her way to the cockpit and sat down in the co-pilot's seat.

Bill Perkin smiled at her. "I am glad you are here."

The plane continued to lose height, coming down to barely one hundred feet above the highway. It bypassed the road to Heronimo, banking at the next turn-off a few miles further on. A sign shaped like an arrow carried the words *Heronimo Airfield*.

Cruising along the highway from the opposite direction, a small battered pick-up truck, a Jeep, took the same turn-off. A jumble of well-used equipment lay in the back of the truck – trapping, fishing, and prospecting gear.

Eileen saw the driver, alone in the cabin upfront, poke his head out of the door window and look up. A man in his sixties, lean and weather-beaten, wearing a dark green safari hat. She waved to him even though she knew she was unseen within the cockpit of the airplane.

The pilot circled the airfield. "It's tight," he said. "Like they told me."

Eileen gave a wry laugh. "Yes. Very."

The landing area was small, a flattened field, pale green in the sunlight. An irregular square, it offered space enough to land for light aircraft, crop-sprayers, four-seaters at most.

There were two buildings. They passed above a large hangar by the roadside and then, at the far end, over a control tower with a diner below. A gritted perimeter track ran along the boundary of the field, with only the stretch outside the diner paved with concrete.

Bill Perkin circled and came in low, close enough to see the windsock. It hung limply. "No help there."

"We will have to pick a diagonal," Eileen said.

"Yeah. But which one?"

"South-east to north-west seems longer."

"How much room have I got do you reckon?"

"About four hundred yards, I'd say." She sighed. "Let's hope it's into whatever wind there is down there."

He circled the airfield again and came in hedge high, touching down immediately in the corner beyond the control tower. The plane bumped across the airfield, slowing but not stopping until they came perilously close to a gate at the northwest corner.

***

Earlier, at mid-morning, Jason Bligh strolled out of the hangar and made his way across the airfield to the diner. The suit he wore was deep blue, the shirt pure white, the only concession to the warmth of the sun, a loosened tie. He was carrying a brown leather case, a piece too small to be called a suitcase, too large to be a briefcase. The impression given by him was that of a business executive *en route* to his office.

The diner carried no name above the door, only an emblem, a picture painted in crimson of the horned head of a bison. There were booths on either side, the bench seats comfortably padded, leading to an open kitchen and a bar with high stools.

Jason sat down in a booth by the window. It gave him a view of the landing field and the hangar, the gritted perimeter track and the short concrete stretch alongside the diner, used for parking by customers. The only vehicle to be seen was a black Ford saloon parked outside, marked *Sheriff Heronimo County* in white on the doors.

The leather case was hinged. He raised the top and took out a map. It was identical to the map given to Eileen Porter on arrival at LAX, but with the obliterated area intact, showing details of mountains in blue, a river, a forest in green.

A man came over with a coffee, his approach was soundless. He was tall, olive skinned, his long black hair plaited into a pigtail. "A hallo from the *Red Buffalo*. I'm the manager, Jimmy Mohawk." He placed the mug of coffee on the table. "Sorry, it's black. The milk has gone sour."

Jason folded the map. "No problem for me, I like my coffee black." He took a sip. "It tastes pretty good."

"Do you want a donut? On the house."

"Just the coffee will do, Mr Mohawk."

"Everybody round here calls me Jimmy."

Jason saw his gaze shift to the window. A pick-up truck, a Comanche jeep, was pulling in behind the sheriff's car. "It seems you have a customer, pal."

There was no reply. The manager of the diner had returned to the open kitchen. He nodded to a large fat man seated on a stool at the bar counter. "Sam."

Sheriff Henry Muller returned Jimmy's nod with a shrug. "I told you he'd be back come first week of April."

The owner of the pick-up truck glanced at Jason when he entered. "Howdy, stranger." Without pausing he strode over to the bar and dumped a woven straw creel on the counter.

Jimmy leaned forward to take a sniff. "I smell fish, Sam."

Sam Konstanz emptied three river trout from the basket. "Fresh as spit. Fry up a treat, Jimmy."

Jimmy put the fish in a plastic container in the fridge. "Today is Thursday. Ham and eggs."

"Are you sure?" Sam frowned and turned to Muller. "Ain't tomorrow Saturday?"

"Not by my reckoning, Sam."

"Heck, seems like I got back a day too soon." His attention returned to Jimmy. "Reckon as how I'll have to settle for them ham and eggs, then."

Jimmy cracked two eggs on the hotplate.

Sam lowered himself onto the stool next to Muller. "What's going on, Sheriff? The President paying us a visit?"

"Hell, no. The guy never stirs out Thursdays." The sheriff looked hard at Sam. "It appears we got us a bunch of juvenile delinquents on a hunting trip." He rolled his eyes at Jason. "The town folk will want me to see them safely out of here."

Sam gave a cackle of laughter. "Reckon that'd go for the President, too."

Jimmy laid a plate of ham and eggs and a bread roll on the counter in front of him. "Find anything, Sam?"

"Not a darn grain." He squashed a piece of roll into the egg yolk. "That river lode is plumb run out."

Henry Muller shook his head. "Jimmy is talking about an airplane. Disappeared around three months back."

"Can't help you there, sheriff. Didn't see me nothing except a heck of a lot of snow and ice." Sam grunted. "Where them juvenile delinquents plan on doing their hunting?"

"From what I hear, it's gonna be your neck of the woods."

Sam let out another cackle. "I hope they ain't expecting on catching something." He looked at the stranger, raising his voice. "That there helicopter of yours would scare a dead tortoise away."

His words were drowned in the noise of an aircraft coming in low. It zoomed upward overhead. "I guess that must be them," Muller said.

All three watched Jason close his leather case and leave the diner.

***

Eileen was first through the boarding door of the airplane. Jason waited for her to reach him, the pilot had taxied close to the *Red Buffalo*. Taking her arm, he walked her away a few paces, Dan Glasson and the teenagers were following her out of the plane. "Any problems?" he asked.

"Yes, I have two. The guards."

"I thought that might get to you. Wait here. There is something I want to show you."

Jason walked back to the airplane. He opened his wallet and gave Dan a few dollar bills. "Here. Buy them all lunch. You have got thirty minutes."

"Only thirty minutes, sir?"

"That's right."

Dan raised the dollar bills in his hand, showing them to the others. "You heard the man. Chow time."

Jason came back to Eileen and took her arm again. "Let's go."

From the air the hangar had looked old and frail to Eileen. Drawing close she wondered that the rusted corrugated iron structure held together at all. One wall was missing entirely. When she saw what lay inside her eyes widened. Most of the space was taken up by a huge military helicopter.

"Is that monster here for us?" she whispered.

"Only the very best will do."

She whistled. "You must carry a lot of clout with your people, Jason."

"Sure. But they want results. Helping kids on minor misdemeanours isn't going to be enough for them."

"I see. You are talking about Raul and Jon."

"Yeah. They make your delinquents seem about as dangerous as Peter Pan and Wendy." He narrowed his eyes. "Is that a problem, too?"

"That depends." She frowned. "I thought the idea was to get the kids out there on their own."

"It still is, that hasn't changed." He shrugged. "Eileen, we have got no goddam choice. The two guards are part of the deal."

"Your people's deal, not mine." Her tone hardened. "My ideas won't work with guards. The kids need to make their own decisions, find their way together."

"Are you sure about that?"

"Yes, I am. Dead sure."

He sighed. "Maybe they'll let us pull the guards after the first couple of days."

She turned away. "No, it has to be now. Or the hike is over."

He followed her out of the hangar. "All right. I'll have another word with my people."

They heard the crack of a rifle shot.

Jason moved past her, drawing a handgun from his shoulder holster. "Let me deal with this."

***

Dan led the way to the diner, the teenagers straggling behind, with Grant Redd at the rear. Raul nudged Jon when they reached the Jeep Comanche pick-up truck. They were the last of the teenagers, the rest had followed Dan into the *Red Buffalo*. "Listen," he said, and imitated the sound of a car engine starting up. "What do you think, *amigo*?"

"Right now, my empty belly is telling me I'm hungry."

"What? You like to eat gringo shit?" Raul switched to Spanish, the guard with the rifle was close. "*La comida en Mexico es mucho mejor.*"

Grant prodded him from behind. "Move it, greaser."

The teenager swung round in a crouch, arms outspread, as if to spring.

The guard took a step back, raising his rifle. "Go ahead. Try me." He eyed Jon. "You too, mother fucker."

Raul straightened. "*Que piensas, amigo?*"

"*Creo que viva Mexico.*"

The pair were lightning fast. Raul kicked at Grant, Jon grabbed the rifle and smashed the butt in the guard's face. They got into the cabin of the pick-up truck, Jon behind the wheel. Raul shorted the wires under the dashboard, and the engine croaked into life. Jon pressed his foot hard on the accelerator. The pick-up truck moved forward jerkily.

Raul shook his head. "*Hombre*! You are going the wrong way."

Jon swung the truck round in a U turn, tyres squealing.

By then Dan had emerged from the diner, the teenagers crowding behind him. He picked up the rifle. "Hold it right there. You hear me?"

The truck accelerated forward.

Dan took careful aim at a rear tyre. Rees watched his finger tighten on the trigger. At the last moment he moved closer, knocking the rifle barrel up with his fist. The bullet flew harmlessly skywards.

Coming out of the hangar, Jason halted. The pick-up was coming towards him with two teenagers upfront. Taking aim with the Colt pistol he fired several times. One shot burst a front tyre, another set the engine aflame. The Comanche pick-up slewed to a standstill. Both teenagers climbed out. Raul shrugged at Jon and raised his arms. Dan was waiting, aiming the rifle.

Jason replaced his revolver in its holster and walked past them. Dan had handcuffed the pair together. He pushed through the excited teenagers outside the diner. The old man and the sheriff were waiting for him at the door.

The old man blocked his way. "Young feller. You just shot up my truck."

He gave the old man a nod of sympathy. "I am sorry. These things happen at times. Your vehicle was being stolen."

The sheriff frowned. "Fact is, Mr Bligh, the law of this State entitles Sam Konstanz here to reasonable compensation."

"Sure, there is no problem with that. I'll process his claim personally." He winked at Sam. "Do it right, Mr Konstanz, and you'll get enough to buy yourself a brand- new jalopy."

"Maybe so. But that old girl and me have been running around together for years and years, and I ain't inclined to let her go. Least, not yet awhile."

Jason gave a shrug. "All right, old timer, have it your way," he said and walked past them into the diner. Eileen was inside, bent over Grant Redd stretched out on a booth seat.

Jason went over to them. The prison guard was groaning, she was gently palpating his temporo-mandibular joint. "Is he going to make it?"

Eileen shook her head. "No. He has a fractured jaw."

"Damn." Jason took out his mobile phone. "I'll have to call my people."

"We should talk first, don't you think?"

He looked around and nodded. "Yeah, I guess so." They were alone in the diner apart from the injured guard. "Let's sit at the bar."

They sat side by side on two of the bar stools. She glanced back at the guard. "I read his report. We are better off without him."

"Okay," Jason said. "But if I tell that to my people, especially after what happened out there, they'll abort the mission. That is for certain."

"Not if you don't call them."

"Listen, there's a problem keeping quiet on the issue. Our party were not the only witnesses to what happened."

Eileen turned her head. They were no longer alone in the diner. "Do you mean those two?" she whispered.

Jason took a quick look and saw that Sam Konstanz and Henry Muller had followed them in. "Exactly," he said. "The truck belongs to the old man. And the fat guy is the town sheriff."

Sam sat down on the stool next to Jason. "We ain't through yet. Where do I send the bill, young feller?"

Jason frowned. "Not now. Can't you see I am busy?"

"How long do you plan on being busy?"

"Give me a break, will you?" Jason turned back to Eileen. "Sorry, it's too big a risk. You know the deal. Two guards. And we are one short."

Eileen shrugged. "Fine. I'm happy with Dan Glasson. All we need is a replacement for the other one."

Jason stared at her. "You'd go along with that?"

"You have my word."

"Okay. But who?"

"Perhaps the sheriff can help." Muller was sitting by the old man. "Did you see what happened. sheriff?" she asked.

"Most of it."

She sighed. "We lost one of our guards. A fractured jaw. Can you recommend anyone?"

Muller jerked his head at the man behind the bar. "How about Jimmy Mohawk there? Nobody knows that wild country better than him."

The old man snorted. "Heck, I knows it better than he does."

"We need a guard, not a guide," Jason said icily.

Muller nodded agreement. "Yeah, no telling who or what you might meet out there." He jerked his head again. "It so happens Jimmy's the darnedest shot we got in these parts. Ain't that the truth, Sam?"

Sam glared at him. "Ain't you forgetting them two years I was in Vietnam? Sharp shooting." He grunted. "Had me an officer the spitting image of this young feller. Same bossy ways, too."

Eileen laughed. "Out there, I'll be in charge."

Sam nudged Jason. "That so?"

Jason gave a reluctant nod.

Sam offered Eileen his hand. "Lady, you just got yourself the best guard this
side of San Petro."

Eileen smiled and shook his hand. She turned to Dan who had brought in the hand-cuffed pair. "Take them off." She got to her feet. "You two left without lunch. You have twenty minutes."

Jason followed her out of the diner.

Freed of the handcuffs, Raul and Jon sat down at the bar. Jimmy cracked four eggs on the hotplate and placed knives and forks and two cans of cola on the bar top in front of them. He pushed a basket of hamburger buns closer. "Help yourself."

Jon picked up his knife and ran a finger along the blade edge.

Sam leaned towards him. "Seeing as how we'll be keeping company, mind
if I ask you something?"

Jon opened the can and took a swig of cola.

"It's nothing personal, boy."

Jimmy placed two plates of ham and eggs on the bar top. Jon used the knife to slide the eggs and ham into a bun. "You sure about that?"

"You got my word."

Jon wrapped a paper serviette around the blade and slipped the knife unseen into his jacket pocket. "I'm listening."

"Why in heck didn't you take the other goddam automobile?" Sam let out a cackle. "The sheriff here is always telling how it's bullet proof."

Jon swallowed a mouthful of ham and egg before answering. "You should have said, old-timer."

"Darn right I should. Next time I will."

FOUR: APACHE WARRIOR

Dark green in colour, the helicopter squatted like a bloated locust on the bare brown earth in front of them. Along with the others Eileen had watched Jason taxi the aircraft out of the hangar through the missing wall. They were all there, the last to join them was Sam and the two teenagers who had stolen his pick-up truck. A rifle was slung over his shoulder, but in a casual manner that gave her no cause for alarm. A rucksack hung from his other shoulder.

She saw him take off his hat and wipe sweat from his brow using a dark red handkerchief. They were standing in blazing sunlight. His face was grizzled, his hair long and grey-white, his clothes an old-fashioned fringed buckskin jacket and Levis, and for a moment she pictured him as a prospector in the Californian gold rush of the 1860's.

Jason's voice brought her back to the present. He was leaning out of the cockpit window above.

"Miss Porter, time to get everybody on board." Her watch adjusted to PST showed close to one o'clock.

She led the way, entering the aircraft through a boarding doorway further along the fuselage. Her experience with helicopters did not include one of this size. It was a twin-rotor military craft, a utility version modified to carry a detachment of troops. The interior was long and wide and rectangular, with two rows of seats facing each other on either side of a central aisle. The seats, their backs to the windows, looked like two lines of dining chairs. There were thirty-six in all.

She watched the teenagers climb inside. Karin and Rees sat together while the others chose to sit separately. Dan was the last of the party to enter, Sam had followed her in. She waited until he closed the door behind him before continuing along the aisle. The main entrance was at the rear, an entryway high enough and wide enough to permit a medium-sized tank to pass, though now ir was blocked by piles of camping equipment, clothing, cans of food and suchlike heaped against the door. She spent a few minutes checking through the items. A batch of sheepskin jackets suggested that they would be heading for somewhere much colder than Heronimo airfield.

The aircraft shuddered; Jason had started the engine.

She retraced her footsteps to the seating area. Karin and Rees were still sitting side by side, but the other teenagers had moved around, Leem closer to Raul and Fara next to Jon.

The helicopter rocked as the twin blades above began to rotate.

Eileen crouched down by Karin. "Are you still nervous?"

The girl nodded. "Yeah, I am, but not as bad I was before."

Rees squeezed her arm. "Stay cool, woman, you will be safe with me."

Eileen became aware that the helicopter was rising.

She chose the first chair in the starboard row, the one facing the entry door on the other side. Beyond her seat the aisle opened directly to the cockpit, giving her a view of Jason Bligh. He turned his head the moment she sat down. "Come on up."

There were two places in the cockpit, Jason was in the pilot seat on the left. She settled into the other next to him, a place normally occupied by a navigator or a lookout.

The helicopter rose steadily. She watched the airfield beneath them shrink to the size of a postage stamp and the town of Heronimo move to only a handbreadth away to the north. The range of mountains seen from the twin-engine aircraft that brought them to the airfield seemed much closer now. At length Jason ended his circling and headed in their direction.

By then she had familiarized herself with the instrument panel. The altimeter showed two thousand feet. Her gaze shifted to him. She remembered seeing a coiled rope in the pile of equipment at the rear. "Jason, is it a mountain climb you have in mind?"

His response was terse. "I'll tell you when we get there."

They hardly spoke. She wondered about him. Clearly Jason was not the person he made himself out to be, someone with a job like her own. She tried to picture Ralph Smithson carrying a gun and shooting at two runaway young offenders. Her imagination failed miserably. Jason's behaviour was more akin to a policeman than a psychotherapist.

Beneath her the scrubland gave way to low foothills that became higher and forested as they drew closer to the mountainous range. She had no idea whether or not he might climb and fly beyond the range until the helicopter hovered over a narrow valley. Two high snow-capped mountains loomed up ahead. "Is this the place?" she asked.

"It could be. Let's take a closer look."

His answer surprised her. "Don't you know?"

"Not yet."

The helicopter lost height and looking down she saw a flattened area directly below. Dust whipped up, blocking her vision, but she felt the aircraft land gently with no more than a slight jar. She heard Jason's voice, he had his earphones on and was talking to his people on the radio.

Sam was waiting for her by the exit door. They climbed down into a peaceful hush. the rotor blades had slowed into silence. They were followed out of the helicopter by the teenagers. Dan emerged last of all.

The two snow-capped mountains faced them.

All at once the rotor blades started up again. Sam pointed to a sheltered area by a large boulder, the noise made speech impossible. Eileen nodded and climbed back into the helicopter.

Jason was off the radio, checking the controls. "My people want me back. They expect some heavy duty explaining from me."

She lowered herself into the navigator seat. "Oh. You mean they know about the injured guard?"

"That's right. The stupid son of a bitch up and told them."

"How? We agreed you and I have the only mobile phones."

"He used the phone in the diner." Jason sighed. "Listen, I'll join you as soon as I can. Will you manage all right without me?"

Eileen snorted. "How can I when I don't know where we are supposed to be going."

"Okay." He reached down for the brown leather case at his side. "Here is where you get the full story from me." He put the case on his lap and raised the lid. "Let's start with this."

He brought out a folded map that she recognised. "Isn't that the one the woman at LA airport gave me?"

"Not quite." Closing the case, he flattened the map fold by fold on the lid. "For your eyes only."

She bent over the map when he reached the blank white area on the copy in the cardboard file. The obliterated detail showed – a mountain range, a river, a lake, in shades of blue, a forested area in green, an expanse of desert in yellow.

She placed her forefinger on the map. "Are they the two mountains we can see from here?"

He glanced through the windscreen. "Yeah. Those two."

Her eyes stayed on the map. "Is that a pass between them?"

"I believe it is."

"You haven't told me yet where the hike is headed."

"San Petro." His finger traced a line from the pass to the Mexican town. "You have five days to get there."

She pointed at the yellow expanse of desert on the map. "How about if we go this way?"

"Mexico?" He grunted. "You'll have a tough time keeping hold of those two runaways of mine. I'd take the mountain pass route if I were you. Safer and quicker."

She folded the map and rose to her feet. "It's not my choice, Jason. The teenagers will decide, not me."

"Okay. But we'll keep in touch."

She left him and climbed down from the helicopter, pulling the entry door shut behind her. The moment her feet touched the ground, the rotor blades speeded up. Through the swirl of dust and debris, she saw that the baggage had been shifted from the aircraft to the sheltered area. Head down, she stumbled over to Sam and Dan. Protected by the boulder, the air was free of dust. Together they watched the helicopter rise and swoop out of sight over a hill.

Dan turned to her. "I thought Mr Bligh was coming with us on this hike of yours."

She gave a shrug. "So did I."

"Holy Moses!" the old man burst out, his tone of voice scornful. "There weren't never no chance of that."

"What are you driving at, Sam?" she asked.

"Two real smart partners I got meself." He cackled. "Either of you two ever see one of them whirlybirds fly off home itself. No, I guess not. And as sure as heck, Mr Bligh ain't gonna leave the durn thing lying around here for the picking."

Dan frowned. "Maybe not. But he should have told us."

Eileen looked at her wristwatch. It showed mid-afternoon almost three o'clock. "How soon will it get dark, Sam?"

"Mighty quick, in these parts."

She beckoned the teenagers, they gathered around her. "This is a good spot.
Sheltered from the wind. Plenty of brushwood to light a fire. What do you say we make camp?"

"Make *what*?" Karin asked.

Leem giggled. "Camp, darling. It means we are having an orgy."

"Not with you, that's for sure."

Eileen led the way over to the baggage. Dan had arranged the items in separate piles. She started with the backpacks. The frames were adjustable, hollow lightweight tubes of aluminium alloy that slotted into each other. The rucksacks were canvas, black, with strapped pockets.

"I won't be needing any of them," Sam picked up a coiled rope. "I'll take care of this instead."

There were nine backpacks in the pile. She handed one to each teenager. "Put them on," she said. It took a while to adjust them all to fit.

Next came a pile of sleeping bags, the kind that had ties to tighten or loosen them. Rolled up, they fitted neatly at the top of the backpack frame.

Eileen bypassed the heaps of camping equipment, moving on to two cartons. The polythene food containers inside one were small, their listed contents the same: six plain biscuits, a slice of smoked ham, a piece of roast chicken, tinned fruit, a bar of dark chocolate. She counted forty-five. "Five each." There were bottles of water and drinking utensils in the other carton, grey metal mugs and flasks with attachments that slotted into the backpack frame.

Sam shoved his share into his rucksack. "Lady, your Mr Bligh ain't ain't too generous with his vittles."

Eileen waited until all the food was stowed before dealing with the clothing, the last of the piles. Jason had spared no expense there. The boots were brown hide, zipped calf-high, the gloves were fur-lined, made of black nappa leather, the jackets were skimmed sheepskin. He had done his homework, everything fitted. The two girls were impressed.

Eileen turned back to the pile of camping equipment. The six tents were identical, each with room enough for two people. She turned to Rees. "Karin needs some help. Will you and Fara show her how to pitch the girls tent?"

"Where do you want it?"

"Everyone gets to choose their spot."

Rees picked up one of the two-man tents and walked away with Karin. Fara stayed. "Do I have to share with that fat lump?"

Raul grinned. "It's okay. Me and Jon will make room for you."

Fara poked her tongue at him, then turned to follow Rees and Karin.

***

At three in the afternoon, the Heronimo sheriff's black Ford saloon was travelling south along the highway. Muller was behind the wheel, his eyes on the road. His gaze lifted to where the mountain range ended in the distance. "Getting close now," he said.

Jimmy Mohawk was sitting up front with him. He made no reply.

Muller shifted in his seat. Trying to have a conversation with a guy next to you who didn't talk was unnerving, made him feel uncomfortable. It was why he had the radio playing, to fill the silence. But that didn't help a great deal because he had to keep the volume low, not blasting the way he liked, because Jimmy hated country and western songs.

He sighed. Apart from the mountain range, there was nothing worth looking at, a vista of rock and scrub, a landscape that he feared would in time become a desert where only insects and lizards survived.

It hadn't always been that way. On the contrary, not too long ago, within his family memory, the rocky plateau had been lush and green, a grassland filled with grazing buffalo and deer.

He allowed his mind to wander.

Back then in the mid-1850's when the first of the Mullers arrived, Heronimo was a tiny settlement, a mix of Mexicans and Indians. There was a church, a couple of places where you could eat or find a place to sleep. His family were amongst the first

Europeans to arrive there, decent farming people. But others kept coming, the worst kind, bandits, gamblers, rustlers – a handy place for a getaway across the border - along with hunters, gold prospectors, drifters who were hardly any better.

A jail was built, a sheriff elected. His name was Tom Muller, and his brother Henry owned a shop close to the newly built hotel. On a Monday in July Henry printed the first copy of *The Heronimo Star*, a newspaper that from then onwards was printed on every Monday of the year, unless the Monday happened to fall on Christmas Day. It was there in the print-shop that he'd seen faded copies dating back to those times. Some carried photos, mainly of people, but also of the town and the locality.

A jolt over a crack in the road returned his mind to the present. Everything had changed, mostly for the worse, after the white folk came. He sometimes thought that they had brought the desert with them.

A short distance ahead the highway angled westwards away from the mountains and around the lake. A spectacular sight but they wouldn't be going that far.

Muller took his eye off the road. "You are looking good, chief. Real scary."

Jimmy smiled. He was wearing buckskins and moccasins, with a tomahawk looped over a shoulder and a hunting knife in his belt.

Muller lifted his foot off the pedal. The car slowed. "We ain't getting any closer than this."

Jimmy reached back and picked up a bow and a quiver of arrows lying on the rear seat.

The sheriff braked and pulled off the road onto a layby. He looked across at the two high-peaked mountains. "I'd say we're about twenty miles away as the crow flies."

Jimmy stepped out of the Ford and without a backward glance, set off at a fast lope.

Watching him, the sheriff had no idea where the belief that he was Apache had come from. A whim that had grown into an obsession. Muller gave a shrug. No matter, the guy served his purpose. He made a U-turn and accelerated back to Heronimo Town.

***

Night fell, the sky pin-pricked with stars. He kept pace in the darkness without the need to see, guided by a sense of direction as natural to him as his other five senses. Each step brought him closer to the ancestral hunting ground of his people. There was a distance to go and a task to be done. It was his tribal duty to protect his homeland from desecration by strangers. The notion intoxicated him. His loping strides became longer, his legs imbued with added vigour. He was a warrior engaged in personal combat.

He had not always known that he was Apache. The knowledge came out of the blue on a morning in San Francisco, the city where his life had been spent. He was hurrying along a dockside street when a man stepped out of the shadows, his hand outstretched, blocking his way on the narrow sidewalk. "Please, help me. Only you will understand."

The man was old, bowed, white-haired, a beggar it seemed. Late for work, he tried to squeeze past him. "Look, I'm broke, no money, like you. Try somebody else."

The beggar's hand tugged at his arm. "Hear me. You are one of my people. My spirit is filled with shame."

He halted, thunderstruck. The beggar had spoken to him in a language that he had never heard spoken before, yet he understood every word.

Before he could respond, the old man had moved on. He was easy to follow, the colourful yellow and green blanket around his head and shoulders stood out, even at a distance in a crowded street.

At length he offered the beggar a dollar. "I have a question. Who were our people?"

The old man's eyes were vacant, greyed by cataracts, but they saw enough to take the money. "We were a tribe of the Apache nation. No warriors were braver in battle."

He took out another dollar bill. "Do you remember where we come from?"

The ancient man took the second dollar. "I tell you, go to Heronimo. There you will find a way to our hunting ground."

He lay awake most of the night searching his memory for clues to his identity. All he knew for sure was that a cop had found him wrapped in a blanket in a street doorway, an abandoned infant. As before, nothing new came to him. But he awoke late in the morning with a vivid image of the blanket in his mind. The colours matched the colours of the blanket around the old man's shoulders, yellow and green. Peering at his face in the mirror above the wash basin he saw the olive skin, the black hair, the piercing stare, of an Apache warrior. He knew who he was and where he came from.

A flicker of light caught Jimmy Mohawk's attention. He had reached the top of a ridge and was looking down at a narrow valley. At once all his senses became fully alert. There was the whiff of wood smoke in the air and the far-off murmur of voices. The flickering light was a campfire.

Following the top of the ridge brought him directly above the camp site but from there his view was blocked by a massive boulder that lay at the bottom. He started down, using footholds and handholds, his descent soundless. Twenty feet above the boulder, the pitted surface became sheer, as smooth as glass. He hung by his fingertips for a moment before dropping. His moccasins made a soft thud. Flattening himself on the boulder, he peered over the edge.

The fire lay at the centre of the camp. The six tents were empty, they were all gathered around the fire, listening to the black hair one softly chord his guitar. Looking down, he recognised him as one of the two who had made off with Sam's pick-up truck. He had served both getaways with ham and eggs at *Red Buffalo*. He remembered their names: Raul, the guitar player, and Jon, the one who had stolen a knife, a steak knife with a serrated blade. Two warriors who failed in a brave attempt to free themselves. Soon they might meet in combat, hand-to-hand.

He saw Sam sitting with the woman and the guard, a little apart from the others. The firelight glinted on the guard's spectacles. A man of small consequence, unable to control the young people in his charge. The woman was a more dangerous adversary, but one he could handle.

His gaze shifted to the teenagers. It might be useful to know how they all related to each other, an indication of how they would behave, who they might protect. Watching, he saw the paleface boy move closer to Raul.

His gaze moved on to the yellow hair girl. She shivered. The dark face boy next to her put an arm around her shoulder. A gesture of protection. He was tall and muscular, more a man than a boy. A worthy opponent.

The red hair girl frowned and shifted away from them to the other getaway. Jon, the silent one, armed with a knife, pretended not to notice her.

Finally, Sam caught his attention.

The old man had brought a harmonica from his jacket pocket. After wetting his lips with his tongue, and a blow from end to end, he played the tune of a song. "Can you play that one, boy?"

The guitar player shook his head. "No. What is it?"

"Shit, everybody knows 'Old Smokey'."

"Not me, *viejo*."

The paleface reached for the guitar. "Here, let me show you."

The guitar player grunted. "*Chico*, if I need your help, I will ask."

"Give it to him, *hombre*," the other getaway said. "We all of us want to hear the song."

The paleface played a few chords, then stopped. "It don't sound right." He shook the guitar.

The guitar player glared at him. "Shit, are you gonna play it or fucking break it?"

The paleface shrugged and started the tune. Sam joined in on the harmonica and all of them sang the words, even Raul the second time around.

He saw the woman stand up when the song ended. "We should call it a night. You will be making an early start in the morning."

He watched them split up and head for their tents. Only Sam stayed by the fire. He lit the cigarette he had rolled.

The yellow hair girl came back and kneeled beside him. "Do you mind me sitting next to you?"

"Heck, no. But how come you ain't in your tent, sound asleep?"

"I can't. I'm dying for a smoke."

Sam laid a few strands of tobacco on a cigarette paper. "Ain't none of your friends got one?"

"They aren't my friends."

He folded the paper into a cigarette, licking the edge down. "I seen the other gal smoking."

"Fara's a bitch. She won't give me one of hers."

He handed the cigarette to yellow hair and lit it with a glowing twig from the fire.

"Thanks, Sam." She took a deep puff. "Gee, that tastes so good."

Listening on the boulder, Jimmy Mohawk turned onto his back and closed his eyes.

At a little before dawn, he was a figure crouched on the large boulder, outlined against the lightening eastern sky. The fire had burned down to a few glowing embers. He dropped catlike to the ground. The camp was silent. Straightening up. he loped, unseen and unheard, into the darkness.

FIVE: DEATH BY DROWNING

Voices woke Eileen. Daylight had come and she could hear Sam and Dan outside her tent, building the campfire. For a while, awake in her sleeping bag, her thoughts went back to the night before.

They had pitched their tents in a circle, the youngsters on one side, the adults on the other, six tents in all. In her mind's eye she saw everyone leave their tent and gather around the campfire that burned at the centre of the site. A while had passed, night had brought a sharp drop in temperature and the fire provided warmth and light. She and Dan and Sam sat hunched on the bare ground close together whereas each teenager chose a spot by the fire closest to their tent as if for protection, but separately, apart from each other.

Lying awake there, Eileen allowed herself a tingle of self-satisfaction. As the night wore on, the youngsters drew closer together and bonded in the manner that she had hoped, each of her three rebels with one of Jason's hard-edged trio.

Comforted, Eileen slid out of the sleeping bag and dressed quickly.

It was bitterly cold outside, the sun hidden behind the mountain range. The two men were drinking tea by a blazing fire. Dan dropped a teabag in her mug and added water boiled in his canteen. She took a sip. "Where did you get the teabag?"

Sam answered. "I grabbed me a handful afore leaving the diner."

The pair watched her drink. "Time to wake them," Dan said after she emptied the last drops of the tea. The teenagers were still asleep in their tents.

Sam snorted. "Them kids ain't getting none of that there tea of mine."

Eileen waited until the youngsters had finished a breakfast of a hard biscuit and a slice of ham. "All done?"

They looked at her sleepy-eyed.

"Right, let's get started on the hike." She crouched to spread a map out on the ground, the one that the woman had given her at LA airport.

All the teenagers except Karin squatted down around her.

She placed her finger beyond Heronimo town, to where the map became white and blank, the detail removed. "The mountain-range." Her finger moved back to the 'X' she had pencilled in. "We are looking at the two peaks from about here."

"Where are we aiming to get?" Jon asked.

"To San Petro." Her finger ran south down to a small town in a yellow area at the bottom. "You have five days to get there."

Raul looked closely at the map. "San Petro is in Mexico?"

"I believe so."

"How far away is this place?"

"That depends. Across the mountains, I would say about a hundred miles away more or less. If you want to avoid the climb, you can take this longer route." Her finger moved west from the 'X' to a small lake where the mountains ended and then southward again into the yellow area and then east to San Petro. "Perhaps an extra twenty-five miles."

Rees frowned. "Who gets to decide, Miss Porter?"

"You do. This is your show." Eileen placed a pocket compass on the map. "You will need this."

Jon looked up at her, she had risen to her feet. "You and the others are just along for the ride?"

"Yes, that is all we are in a manner of speaking, observers." She turned away back to Dan and Sam, leaving them.

They stayed crouched around the map. Leem eyed the two looming mountains. "No chance of me climbing one of those heaps of fucking rock."

"Use your eyes, man," Rees said. "There ain't no need to climb either of them." He pointed a finger at where the two mountain slopes met. "A god given sign, my people. A pussy-hole pass goes right between them."

They all stared up at the two mountains.

"All I see is fucking snow," Raul said. "How do we know if this pass of yours is blocked?"

"How are we gonna know if it ain't?"

Raul eyed Jon. "What do you think, *compadre*?"

Jon shrugged and rose to his feet. "Why ask me?"

Karin was silent until they were all standing with her. "Well, I'm for walking no further than we have to."

Fara looked her up and down. "The shape you are in, that's no surprise."

"What are you getting at, skinny ass?"

Rees raised his hand. "Bros, we're all together, equals in this fix. Let's do it right and take a vote. Okay?" Nobody answered. "Right. Ladies first."

Raul turned around. "I don't see no lady here."

"Hey, come on, rude boy. Be polite." Rees faced Karin. "Which way for you, girl?"

She gazed at the mountains. "That-a-way. I guess I fancy the view."

Fara glared at her. "Well, I don't."

Leem sighed. "Listen, I won't make a habit of it, but this time I am of the same mind as skinny arse."

Fara snorted. "Because you are shit scared of heights, slobber-mouth."

"I am not so keen on them either," Raul said. "That make three of us." He spoke to Jon. "*Vamos a Mexico, compadre.*"

Rees eyed Jon. "Are you with them, bro?"

Jon shook his head. "Not me."

"Why not. *amigo*?" Raul asked.

I have seen that desert. Nothing but rock and sand and salt flats. It is no place to be." He turned to Rees. "Three to two. Your call, brother."

"Man, I'm for taking a look at the pass." Rees grunted. "Seems like it's three votes each way."

Listen," Karin said. "We are all city people, strangers out here except Jon. I say we give him two votes.

"You mean, make him leader?" Leem said.

Raul nodded and eyed Jon. "What do you say, *compadre*?"

"Cool it. That isn't my style. Get somebody else to play the part."

"What about you then, Raul?" Leem asked.

"Are you crazy?" He twanged his guitar. "I only play this."

"That's me out, too," Leem said. "Anyway, I ain't the type."

They all looked at Rees. "That leaves just you, pal," Jon said.

Rees shrugged and picked up the map and compass.

An hour later he helped Karin put on her backpack, the campsite had been cleared, the tents and the gear packed. "We all set, people?" There was a murmur of excitement from the rest. He turned away. "All right then. Let'sgo."

Eileen, Sam and Dan watched them set off. "They are headed for the mountains, Miss Porter," Dan said.

"Their choice. The right one, wouldn't you say, Sam?"

"I ain't that sure." Sam narrowed his eyes. "There's some mighty tough country out there."

"That's the whole idea. It will bring out the best in those kids."

"What do you have in mind for us?"

"We trail them. Close enough to know what is going on."

Dan grunted. "Five bucks says they don't make it."

Sam shook his head. "Not me, feller. I ain't in the habit of throwing money away."

"How about you, Miss Porter?"

"Dan, you have yourself a bet."

***

At around mid-morning Rees halted. They had reached the edge of an embrasure that was too wide and too deep to cross. He turned to Jon. "We need to take a look from above."

They climbed back to the top of the slope. From there they saw that the embrasure narrowed to the right. Re-joining the others, they led the way to a point at which the embrasure became a crevice narrow enough for them to step over.

Rees looked up at the twin peaks towering above them. The gap where their slopes met, his direction throughout, was blocked from view by one of the mountains. His eyes scanned the rock face and picked out a ledge that ran diagonally upwards. "Here is where we start to climb."

Reaching the ledge Rees kept going, edging along whenever there was barely enough space for someone with a backpack to pass. In that manner he rounded a bulge in the rock. Beyond the bulge the ledge widened considerably. Jon and Raul and Leem were close behind. Their speed picked up.

The two girls lost sight of them. Fara tried to edge past Karin. "You are too slow we are falling behind."

Karin squeezed herself flat against the rock face. "Careful, now."

Stretching out, Fara stumbled. Karin instinctively grabbed her arm, but the girl tried to jerk free. "Let go of me, you fat cow."

Karin released her hold abruptly. She saw Fara step back, lose her footing, teeter, fall…

Further back on the ledge they heard a scream. "Rees! REES!"

"It's Karin," Eileen said.

Sam was the first to reach her. She had her back to the rock face, a hand across her mouth, unable to speak. "What happened to the other one?"

She pointed.

Sam knelt, his hands on the ledge, and peered down. A rock sill jutted out a few yards below. The girl was on the edge, shrinking away from a rattlesnake.

Sam's voice was a hoarse whisper. "I guess you must've disturbed he critter. Keep still now. Not a sound." He climbed down agilely to the outcrop. The snake had not moved. Using his rifle, he flicked the creature over the side. "You all right, girl?"

She uttered a sob and rose to her feet. "I slipped. I am sorry."

"Heck, there ain't no call for apologising. Looking out for you kids is what me and Dan is getting paid for."

Fara began to climb back to the ledge. Karin and Eileen reached down for her. She scowled at Karin and took Eileen's hand.

Out of sight ahead Rees followed a curve in the ledge. A pass came into view, the one he had hoped for. It was still some distance away, beyond a deep gorge in the mountainside. A few paces further on, where the ledge widened, he took off his pack and sat down. Raul and Jon slumped by him, their backs against the rock.

Rees unscrewed the metal flask attached to his backpack his mouth was dry. "What say we take a break?"

Leem was the next to reach them. He was panting. "Ain't…ain't that the pass?"

Nobody answered him.

He slumped down with the others. "Shit, you got it right, Rees."

One by one the rest caught up, Eileen, Sam, Dan, the two girls last of all. Karin sat close to Fara. "It was my fault back there," she whispered. "I am real sorry."

"You are lying, bitch, you did it on purpose." Fara got to her feet. "Keep away from me, will you."

Leem looked up at her. "What is the matter with you two?" Both stayed silent.

Eileen felt the buzz of her phone. She moved out of earshot to answer.

The caller was Jason Bligh. He was sitting in the cockpit of the helicopter, parked in the rusty hangar. "How are the troops making out?"

"Fine. We are coming up to the pass. What is happening at your end, Jason?"

He reached for the bottle of bourbon he kept in the leather suitcase. "I'm with my people right now."

"In Los Angeles?"

"That's right." He poured a drink. "They are raising hell."

"Oh. What will they do?"

"Not a goddam thing. But it's going to take a while to convince them." He swallowed the bourbon in a gulp. "Listen, I'll call you back when I know more."

Eileen frowned. Jason had ended the call.

***

Jimmy Mohawk crouched on the rock spur; the expedition party had come into sight on the far side of the gorge. The spot he had chosen thirty metres above the gorge gave him a view of a log-pile upstream and a waterfall downstream. Though it was early afternoon and the mountainside cast in shadow, he stayed crouched, watching them gather at the edge.

They looked down apprehensively, the river at the bottom had been hidden from their view. Swollen by melting snow, the mountain stream was at its widest, a surging flow of water thirty metres wide. The sides of the gorge were sheer slippery rock.

"Sod you, Rees," Fara said. "I told you we should've gone the other way."

"It's too late for that now, girl. We'd never make San Petro in time."

Raul spat into the river. "Who gives a shit."

"Ain't that why we are all here?"

"*Hombre*, this water will sweep us away like feathers. Nobody told us this is why we are all here."

"Fucking right," Leem agreed. "We've got no chance carrying all this camping stuff."

"Well, I ain't leaving without giving it a try," Rees said. He unshouldered his backpack. Jon followed suit.

Karin wriggled out of hers. "I guess we need to take another vote." She looked at each of them in turn. "Who is for turning back?" Fara, Leem and Raul raised their hands. "Three of you."

She raised her own hand. "Well, I'm for giving the river a go. Is that your way of thinking, Jon?"

He nodded. "Your call again, boss."

"Right on." Rees high-fived with Jon and Karin. "Okay. But me first."

Sam uncoiled the rope he was carrying and tossed an end to Rees. "Reckon you'll be needing a little help crossing over, son."

Rees knotted one end of the rope around his chest, Sam looped the other end around a boulder. Jon and Karin lowered him into the gorge, the water reaching his waist.

He started towards the far side of the gorge forty or more paces away. The water rose higher around him at every step. Eileen stayed with Sam who was playing out the rope. Halfway across the gorge with the water at chest level Rees vanished from sight, dragged under.

Eileen tried to grab the rope, to haul him in.

"Leave him be." Sam played out more rope. "The kid will make it."

She saw Rees surface.

Jimmy Mohawk was watching him from above. At times his gaze had shifted from the dark face boy to the log pile half a mile upstream. Now his eyes stayed fixed on him swimming powerfully against the downflow. He waited, crouched, for the dark face one to reach the bank below before straightening up and leaving the rocky spur.

Rees unknotted the rope around his chest and, keeping it almost taut, looped the end several times around a rock overhang on the bank. The rope stretched a little fabove the water to the far side. A tug showed it to be straight and secure. The others were waiting. He raised an arm to beckon them.

"How do we do this, *hombre*?" Raul asked.

Jon put his backpack on. "We do it together."

He took the lead. With one hand on the rope, he lowered himself into the water. He was carrying Rees's backpack as well as his own. The two girls were next, freed of their backpacks by Leem and Raul. He gripped Fara's hand. "All of you, keep a hold of the rope, and of each other."

Out of sight of them Jimmy reached the pile of logs, the trunks of maple and fir trees chopped down by him and assembled before the snows came. They were tied together at the edge of the gorge. He moved swiftly. Tomahawk in his hand, he hacked through the ropes, releasing the logs into the surging water. They rolled in on top of each other, some of them end on.

Downriver, Dan was watching the teenagers help each other up onto the bank on the far side. "Those kids did real good, Miss Porter," he said.

"Bloody good. Now it's our turn to get wet." She shouldered her pack. "Are you going to be all right, Sam?"

"Heck, I got ten bucks says I beat the pair of you across."

"You got yourself a bet," Dan said. "I'll put in my five."

"Lady, how about you?"

Eileen smiled. "Not me, old timer."

Rees was the first to see the logs heaving and churning downriver, he had clambered to a high point. Seconds later they swept Eileen and the two men away. The three disappeared hidden from his view beyond a bend in the gorge. Climbing higher he reached the rock spur on which Jimmy had crouched. From there he followed the line of the gorge to a waterfall and a stretch of water beyond that he took to be the lake seen on the map.

Jon stood beside him. "Any sign of them?"

Rees shook his head.

They clambered down to where the rest were waiting at the edge of the gorge. "What did you see from up there?" Raul asked

"The same as you, bruv." Rees sighed. "Sorry. After the logs hit, I couldn't spot any of them."

Karin shuddered, her voice a whisper. "Do you think they are...all of them are...?" She stopped speaking, unable to put her dread into words.

Rees gave a shrug.

Raul answered. "*Chica*, for sure they are all dead. Nobody can live through that."

"You don't know Miss Porter the way we do, big mouth," Fara said, hiding her fear of the worst. "Isn't that right, Leem?"

"Yeah, Miss Porter always comes through, no matter what. Right, Rees?"

"Man, I don't know." He looked up at the darkening sky. "It's getting late. We had better find some place to camp." He turned to Jon. "How about you watch out up there for a bit longer? Just in case."

"Sure thing."

"You want me to keep you company, *amigo*?" Raul said.

Jon made no answer but they both began to climb. The rest headed up the narrowing pass.

Coming out onto the rock spur, Raul shifted the guitar from behind his shoulder. "You watch, I will play and sing,"

Jon squatted down close by the edge. "Okay. But not too loud."

After a while spent fingering chords and strumming, Raul began to sing *Cielito Lindo*. His voice was hoarse, unmusical, out of tune with the guitar. A series of other tunes followed, of which Jon recognized none.

Eventually, his repertoire exhausted, Raul returned to *Cielito Lindo*. Day had turned with suddenness into night. The moon showed full, the stars a faint scattering across the sky.

"You played that one before," Jon said. He was on his haunches, his eyes fixed on the distant silvery lake.

Raul stopped strumming. "I think we have hung around here long enough."

Jon made no response.

Raul sighed. "*Hombre*, they are dead."

"Is that what you reckon?"

"*Si, es cierto.*"

"How come you are so sure?"

Raul frowned and moved closer. He followed Jon's gaze to a flickering point of light by the lake. "What is that?"

"A campfire, I'd guess."

"Do you think it is them?"

"Could be."

"*Mierda*. That bitch never gives up."

"Who cares? We have got a day's start on them."

"If Rees knows, he will make us wait for her."

"Yeah, he might try." Jon straightened up. "That's why we are not gonna tell him."

***

Sam halted when they were almost half-way across the stream. Eileen was next to him, one hand on the rope, Dan a pace ahead of them. "Anything wrong, Sam?" she asked, her voice a shout in the din.

He raised his hand. "Listen! You hear that?"

"Do you mean the kids?" The youngsters were cheering them on from the far bank.

"No, lady, I don't."

Listening hard, her ears caught a roar above the cheering and the onrush of water. "Any idea what the noise might be?"

"Could be a bunch of logs heading downriver."

"I don't fall for those kind of poker tricks, Sam," Dan said and pushed on. "I aim to win that bet."

An instant later Eileen saw a huge log rise a short distance away upstream. Her first impulse was to follow Dan to the far bank, but Sam tugged her arm. The roar had become a crashing noise, massive logs were tumbling and rearing towards them. "Let go of the rope. Let the river take you."

She let go and the river took her.

The backpack dragged her down. Wriggling out, her head above water again, she saw the logs burst through the rope. One struck Dan. Sam had been swept further away. He was holding on to a log with both arms, the rucksack on his shoulder. The gorge narrowed bringing him nearby. He grabbed her, and she clung to the log with him.

The flow of water funnelled through the gorge speeded up, intensifying the noise of rushing water around her, but gradually she became aware of a sound coming from ahead, a pulsing throb that grew louder. Sam was listening with her. "Time to climb aboard," he said. By then the rushing water had become a torrent.

They hauled themselves up on to the log. She recognised the sound. "Is that a waterfall?"

"Yep."

"How big a drop?"

"Heck, I ain't ever measured the fall but I'd say maybe four houses high. Does that scare you?"

"No, I've dived in from higher. How about you?"

"Lady, the fall ain't the scary bit."

"Then what is it that scares you?"

"Getting hit on the way down."

The log swung broadside on, giving her a view of a lake below. They jumped clear together. She entered the lake feet first, a split second ahead of the log tumbling down in the water cascade behind.

Sam surfaced close by her. They swam to the lake shore, a flat reedy area. She lay on the muddy ground too exhausted to speak.

Sam cackled. "Seems we ain't the first ones here." The body of Dan was afloat, tangled amongst the reeds.

Eileen staggered to her feet.

"Ain't no use, lady." Sam let out another cackle. "That's one feller won't be paying his dues. Not down here, anyways."

His cackle of laughter shocked her. "You are a heartless old so-and-so."

"Yeah, heartless, that's me," Sam agreed. "Reckon I got accustomed to seeing dead bodies lying around me in Vietnam."

Eileen was reminded of Teheran. "Yes, I know what you mean." She sighed. "What next then?"

"We dry out. Gets mighty cold at night."

She helped him gather dead leaves, dry reeds, fallen branches. Somehow or other he had kept a hold on his rucksack throughout. He reached inside for a cigarette lighter. "I've had this longer than I can remember, soon after my first smoke, I guess. Ain't never let me downyet." The small heap of leaves and twigs smouldered and flamed.

Eileen brought out her mobile phone. Water-sodden and useless, she tossed it away.

Sam added branches, and the smouldering heap became a blazing fire. She took off her wet clothes and boots and laid them out on a fallen tree branch to dry. By then night had fallen.

Naked, crouching close to the fire, she asked, "Do you think they can see us from up there?"

Sam grunted. "Right now, I ain't much concerned about them." He was in his underpants and vest. "But if you mean this here fire, lady, they sure can spot it. That's if they're all of a mind to be looking." He poked hard at the fire. "Some of them might still be hankering for Mexico."

"That is what worries me, Sam." Her underclothes were dry. She began to dress.

"You want we should head back for town?" Sam asked her. "Put Sheriff Muller on to them?"

Eileen shook her head forcefully. "No way. Those kids are *my* responsibility." She glanced at him, he was on one leg, putting his trousers on. "Not yours, Sam. You don't have to come up there with me."

"Never had no such intention. Seen me enough of them there mountains lately." He cackled. "Mind, the desert ain't no stroll in the park neither."

She looked hard at him. "Could we catch up with them, going that way?"

"It ain't something I'd care to guarantee." He handed the sheepskin jacket to her. The inside was still damp. "But sure as heck they'd be long gone afore we reached them doin' it the other way."

Eileen put on the sheepskin jacket, zipped the leather boots, and followed him into the darkness.

SIX: EYES LIKE A CAT

Karin's eyes opened. A thin strip of daylight showed that she was alone in the tent. Fara had gone, leaving the flap unzipped. She slid out of the sleeping bag relieved that the girl was not there to see her naked. Her clothes were dry, her boots still a little damp. She dressed quickly and pushed the tent flap wide.

Fara was standing a few paces away with her back to her. It was early morning, the sky misted over, the others still asleep in their tents. They had pitched the camp in darkness where the pass narrowed, close by the rock face, using fallen debris, small chunks of rock, to pin the tents in place.

She saw Fara's shoulders heave and heard a muffled sob. Last night they had hardly spoken to each other. Cold, wet, exhausted they climbed into their sleeping bags without exchanging a word. Now she moved close to her. "What are you doing out here, Fara? Are you okay?"

The girl answered without turning. "I couldn't sleep."

"I couldn't sleep either. I guess we are all of us upset about Miss Porter."

Fara shivered. "Shit, it's freezing."

Karin put an arm around her. "Here," she said and offered a handkerchief:

Fara shoved her away. "Piss off, will you."

"I am only trying to help, honey."

"I don't need any. Not from you, not from anybody." She faced Karin angrily. "And don't ever call me honey again, you fat cow..." She stopped short, her eyes widening in horror.

Karin followed Fara's gaze. Her scream echoed in the narrow pass. A large dead bird was draped over their tent.

The scream aroused the sleepers. They hurried over to them half-dressed and gathered around rhe tent. The bird was large and black, he wings widespread, six feet from tip to tip, the beak pink and hooked.

Rees looked at Jon. "What kind of bird is that?"

"It's a buzzard, a kind of vulture."

"How the fuck did the thing end up there?" Leem asked.

Jon's eyes tracked up the rock face. "The son of a bitch must have flown straight into the mountain."

Rees frowned. "Shit, man, it was a clear night."

"I guess he just wasn't looking."

Rees turned to the two girls. "Either of you hear anything?"

They shook their heads.

"Nothing? No noise?" Jon asked.

Neither of the girls answered.

Jon narrowed his eyes at them. "Not a sound? Are you sure?"

Raul gave a shrug. "What do you expect, *compadre*? They were both asleep like us."

"Yeah, but the bird fell on *their* tent, not on ours." Jon spread his arms apart like wings. "How come the impact didn't wake them?"

Raul lifted the bird. "This son of a bitch is made of feathers, no? Maybe it float down." He hurled the buzzard high in the air. "Listen." It landed on the tent with a resounding thump. He gave another shrug. "Okay. The stupid creature fall asleep there, and then it freeze to death."

"So will we, if we stand around here chatting any longer." Rees pulled the bird off the girls' tent. "Pack up, we are moving out."

"Where are we heading, boss?" Raul asked.

"San Petro." Rees folded the bird's wings. "Unless you want to try getting back across that river without a rope."

"Not me, boss."

Rees carried the buzzard by the legs to a pile of debris a few paces away. Jon followed him. Rees sighed and laid the dead bird on the ground behind the debris. "Nobody will ever know how he got here."

Jon crouched beside him. "Mind if I take a look?" He lifted the bird's wings. An arrowhead was buried in the ribcage, the shaft snapped clean.

Rees grunted. "I was wrong. Now we know what brought him down."

Jon eyed him, putting a finger to his lips.

Rees nodded. "Yeah, bro, you're right. We'll keep this just between the two of us."

At midmorning they passed by drifts of snow piled against the walls of the pass. The mist had cleared, the warmth of the sun above glistening the snow's surface. The drifts widened and deepened as they climbed higher, filling the pass from side to side with unbroken whiteness.

Rees came to a halt, the snow reached above his knees. He was in the lead with Jon and Raul following in his footsteps. Looking back, he realised that the girls and Leem had slowed and fallen almost out of sight behind them. "Listen, let's take a breather."

Jon glanced at Raul. "I don't need one. How about you?"

"I feel good, *compadre*. It look like you are outvoted, boss."

"No, I'm not," Rees responded. "You gave me two votes, remember?"

"*Hombre*, we go quicker without them."

"Listen, we started out on this together. And that's how we are gonna finish." Rees turned to Jon. "What's our hurry anyway? Miss Porter gave us five days to get there."

"Sure. But the lady isn't around any longer."

"All the more reason to stick together. We owe that much to her."

"I don't owe anybody anything." Jon's tone was bitter. "And that includes your Miss Porter."

"We all of us do, bro. She gave us the chance to show we are..." Rees paused. "To show we are people you can trust, who stick to their word. Know what I mean?"

"Man, do you think *us* is what this is all about? A bunch of delinquents?" Jon's voice became scornful. "How dumb can you get."

"Listen, I dig her," Rees said, his manner defensive. "She is straight, no angles. I ain't letting Miss Porter down."

"Maybe I'm not talking about her."

Rees frowned. "Who, then?"

Raul gave Rees a nudge. "Boss, they are coming."

"Good." Rees looked back, Leem and the two girls were still struggling through the snow to reach them. He faced Jon again. "Are you saying Mr Bligh set us up?"

"You saw him. Kind of quick with a gun to be in juvenile rehab, wouldn't you say?"

Raul pointed a finger. "Hey, boss, take a look. The ones we wait for have stopped coming."

Rees frowned. Leem and the two girls were huddled together still a distance away. "Wait here," he said and turned back to them.

They were trying to light a cigarette, but the narrow pass acted like a wind tunnel. Rees snatched the lighter from Fara. "That ain't right. You are keeping us hanging around for you."

"Shit, we need a fag." She tried to grab the lighter. "Give it back."

"Not till we get to the top of the pass and see what's on the other side."

"Gee, Rees, how far is that?" Karin asked.

"I've got no idea." He took her arm. "Let's go find out."

"Up the wall! I'm having a smoke," Fara said.

Karin freed herself. "It's okay. We'll catch you up."

Rees shrugged. "You'd better be quick. Those two ain't gonna hang around for you much longer."

They watched him return to Raul and Jon. Without a backward look, the three started up the pass.

"Fuck! The sods are leaving us here, Fara," Leem muttered.

She scowled. "Not with my lighter. It's the only one I've got."

***

The top of a high ridge gave Eileen a view of an arid rock plateau that stretched unbroken into the far distance. She knew at once that they had reached the desert. Her gaze shifted to Sam, standing beside her. He had taken off his safari hat and was wiping sweat from his brow with his large red handkerchief. "As you told me, Sam, this is no picnic."

He cackled a laugh. "Just so long as we ain't a meal for them pair of ugly critters up there."

She looked at the two vultures circling high overhead. Her laugh was rueful. "They wouldn't enjoy us. We'd be much too tough for them."

"Well, sure as heck I am."

"Are you worried about me then, old timer?"

"I reckon not." He shielded his eyes. "That sun will be high pretty soon." Replacing his hat, he moved on. Eileen followed him. It had become her habit.

Leaving the fire by the lake still alight behind them, he led the way into darkness. She had stayed with him, trusting his sense of direction, impressed even more by the old man's strength and stamina. Their moment standing together facing the desert had been the only time they had paused to rest since setting out.

The route he took showed no sign of human habitation, an area of shrubs and undergrowth, with an occasional clump of trees. Their headway had seemed direct and rapid to her, though it was impossible to be sure without a distant object visible to judge by.

Dawn had come early, unrestricted by the mountain range. Until then she hadn't realized that the trees and shrubs had gone, the grass underfoot replaced by stony ground. "Is this the desert we are in, Sam?" she asked.

"Not yet, lady. You will know soon enough when we get there."

They kept going at walking pace for a while, not slowing until the ground ahead sloped upwards to form what she took to be a high ridge. It was a long hard climb to the top. There she saw that the ridge was a plateau. They stood on the edge of the desert.

Close up, what had appeared to be a flat and even landscape from the top of the ridge was split by fissures and clefts, some deep and wide enough to form canyons, the gradients slippery with grit and pebbles. Their progress was slow and tortuous, but still they pressed on, Sam leading the way.

At length, he veered towards a large boulder, glaring white under a sun which by then had moved almost directly above them. "Time to rest up."

Although close to exhaustion, she felt compelled to carry on, time was running out. "If it's me you're worried about, Sam, I'd much rather keep going."

"I reckoned as how you might be thinking that way, catching up with them delinquents, and all." He slumped down in the shade of the boulder. "Lady, we ain't gonna get nowhere in this heat. Except cook us a little for them there ugly critters." He closed his eyes. "Grab yourself some shuteye. We'll be shoving off again come sundown."

Eileen sighed wearily and sat down next to him.

***

Rees was the first of them to reach the top of the pass. At midday the sun overhead shone on a vista of a widening expanse of white snow sloping down towards a dark green spread of forest that stretched as far as he could see.

Entranced, he turned to beckon the others. "Be cool, people. Come and have a look."

They clustered around him. Karin was closest. "Wow, is that a sight to see or is it not?"

"Yeah, the sort I've been hoping for."

"Almost worth the trouble of getting up here," Leem said.

Fara moved closer to Jon. "The forest looks so peaceful."

"Maybe it only seems that way."

Raul grunted. "How long do we stand here and look, boss? I think we freeze to death like that bird."

"Right on," Leem agreed. "I say we go down there and make ourselves one huge fire."

"Go ahead," Rees said. "Lead the way."

Leem stepped back a pace. "Shit, Rees, why me? You brought us up here."

"That's right, I did." Rees shielded his eyes. "Now I'm looking for a way of getting us down from here."

They all peered with him at the uneven blanket of snow covering the mountainside. Jon broke the silence. "Over there." He pointed. "Beyond the snowline."

Rees followed the direction of his finger. "What am I looking for?"

"Can't you see, a kind of track. I guess it must run under the snow to the pass, to where we are."

Rees frowned. "I don't see nothing." He looked at the others. "Do any of you?" None of them answered. "How about you show us the way, bro?"

"Okay," Jon said and stepped past Rees. "Follow me."

He picked his way down with Rees and the others close behind. His descent was steady and sure-footed, the snow was newly fallen, barely more than ankle-deep. He turned to Rees when they reached the snowline with no more than an occasional drift left between them and the forest edge. "Which direction are we headed?"

Rees brought out the pocket compass. He watched the needle come to rest. "South."

At early afternoon, the sky cloudless and the sun still high, they entered the forest. The tall trees, mostly pine and fir, shut out the sunlight and their view of the mountain range. A sprinkling of snow lay on the ground and the temperature felt noticeably colder. Rees urged them on. "We don't stop till we are well clear of the mountain."

Karin sighed. "How are we gonna to know that?"

"I'll tell you. The ground under your feet will stop sloping."

They kept moving due south. The air grew warmer, the snow disappeared, and the forest became a mix of deciduous trees, oak, elm, ash, the undergrowth patched with flowering plants and tufts of grass.

Rees and Jon stayed together ahead of the others. All at once Jon came to a standstill, his hand raised. Ahead, through the trees, a young deer, a calf, could be seen head down in a glade, nibbling the grass. Jon's voice was low. "I'll circle back of him. Give me a couple of minutes." He vanished into the forest.

The rest of the group found Rees crouched behind a tree. He waved them down.

"What is it?" Karin whispered.

"Take a look."

She smothered a gasp. "Oh my! Gee, isn't she cute?"

Rees waited for Leem and Raul to have sight of the deer. He kept his voice to an undertone.

"Spread out. Not a sound. And don't make a move till I do."

They crept into the undergrowth on either side of him.

Fara frowned. "Where is Jon?"

"Coming up from behind."

Karin clutched his arm. "Rees, you're not going to harm that poor little thing."

"The way me and Jon sees it, she is dinner."

"You mean, eat her?" Fara hissed. "That is disgusting!"

"Stay quiet, you two." The two girls backed away from Rees.

He crept stealthily towards the deer, urging Leem and Raul forward on either side. The young animal raised its head, started away in alarm. Jon leaped to one side and grabbed the creature around the neck. Rees ran forward and they wrestled her to the ground. Jon took a firmer hold.

The two girls heard the snap of the animal's neck. Karin uttered a sob. Fara reached out and squeezed her hand. They were both in tears.

***

The boulder cast a longer darker shadow in the setting sun.

Sam sat down by Eileen. She lay on her side in the shade, still asleep. He swallowed a mouthful of water from the flask and shook her gently. "It's time to move on, lady. The sun's down."

Eileen sat up.

"Here." Sam gave her the flask and watched her take a swallow. "How are you feeling?"

Eileen handed back the flask. "I'm not sure yet." She tidied her hair, using her fingers. "I must look a real mess."

"I'd say you look mighty good, considering. Anyways, out here there ain't no one gonna see you except me." He offered a biscuit. "Reckon you must be feeling kinda hungry."

"Famished. Thanks, Sam."

He waited for her to finish chewing before offering the flask of water again. "Go easy. We got ourselves a-ways to go yet."

"I'll save a drink for later then." She got to her feet. "I'm ready. Which direction?

Sam had straightened up with her. He pointed. "We keep going that way for a while, and then head in till we get to the forest." He grunted. "We get there, it ain't gonna be no cake walk picking up on them kids trail."

She used the setting sun as a guide. "You mean we travel south and then east."

"Yeah, more or less."

"How will you know the way in the dark?"

"Instinct, I suppose."

She laughed. "Like a homing pigeon."

"Heck, if it was my home I was aiming to get to, I'd be headed in the opposite direction."

Eileen looked hard at him. "We'll find them, won't we? We have got to."

He put his hat on, lowering the brim, before meeting her gaze. "Lady, you are damn right we will. I ain't come this far to miss out on us and them kids meeting up together."

She felt reassured. Sam was a man whose word she could trust.

***

They set up a campsite in the glade, the three tents a triangle at the centre. The campfire was closer to the trees, where leaves, twigs and thicker branches lay fallen on the ground. They used Fara's cigarette lighter to set the pile of leaves and twigs aflame. By then night had fallen. It took a while longer before the thicker tree branches merged into glowing embers.

Jon had used the knife taken from the diner to skin, gut and behead the deer calf. Tied to a straight piece of tree branch, he and Rees placed the carcass above the fire. Leem and Raul watched them whereas the two girls faced away, sickened by the smell of roasting flesh.

Flames of burning fat sprang up from the embers. Jon waited for them to die away before tasting a piece of flesh cut from the shoulder. "It's done," he said. In turn the four of them sliced meat from the haunches of the animal, passing the knife to one another. They sat down together, cross-legged, to eat.

"Karin, this tastes good," Rees called. "You should try some."

"I'm not hungry," she responded without turning her head.

Raul grunted. "*Chica*, you think the deer mind who eat her now?"

Fara turned to glare at him. "Leave us be, you creep. We don't want any." She took out a crumpled pack that held two cigarettes and gave one to Karin.

"Are you sure?" Karin said. "Are they your last ones?"

"Go on. Share and share alike."

They put the cigarettes to their lips. Fara lit Karin's cigarette and then her own. Both girls inhaled deeply.

"Gee, Fara," Karin said, "I had you all wrong."

"No, you didn't. I can be a ratty bitch. Even with the best of company."

"Which I am not. Right?"

"Nor me, for that matter. That's why we are both here."

Karin's laugh was rueful. "Hell, I guess at least we have that in common. Neither of us is an angel."

Fara gave a shrug. "What did they get you for?"

Karin frowned. "You mean, why did the cops pick me up?"

"Right on. But only if you want to tell us."

Karin looked round and realized that the others were watching and listening. She tossed her hair at them. "For nothing. That's what."

Raul looked upward, his hands together as though in prayer. "If you are listening, I say we all of us down here are innocent."

Rees laughed. "Ain't that true, bro." He and Raul exchanged high-fives.

Fara turned to face them. "Well, the cops took me in with no good reason."

"You gonna tell us why, *chica*?"

"Yeah. For using a credit card." She giggled. "I said the ugly hag left it for me instead of a tip."

"Were you a waitress?" Jon asked.

"Yeah. Unpaid. Working for my dad."

"You should've known better. The fuzz never believe a word they hear from a waitress."

Raul grunted. "*Compadre*, they believe *una chica* if she say it on the house."

"Well, they believed my bloody dad. It was him who told them." Fara shrugged. "The sod spots me sneaking in with all this great designer stuff." She stood up and struck a pose. "I've still got the leather jacket."

Jon appraised her. "Hey, you look kind of pretty in the one you've got on."

She smiled at him. "How about you, then. What made the cops pick you up?"

"Drug trafficking."

Leem raised his hand. "They got me for that too."

Fara snorted. "Piss off, Leem, you were just a kiddie school pusher." She sat down by Jon. "I bet you were big time. What was it? Coke?"

"Yeah." He turned to Raul. "How about you, *compadre*?"

"*Hombres,* you will not believe this." Raul got to his feet, all eyes on him. "Okay, I tell you." His accent had thickened. "Early one morning I come out of my shitty place, and what do I see?" He opened an imaginary door and peered out. His eyes widened. "A fantastico green Porsche. Such a car I think maybe not safe in el barrio. So I think I better take the car somewhere, keep it safe."

Everyone laughed.

Raul crouched, pretended to turn a key, and made the sound of a car starting up. He shrugged. "How do I look if the tank gonna run out of gas? *Estupido*. A car like that, you fill her up." He glared at Leem. "Right to the top, no?"

"Definitely," Leem agreed.

Still crouching Raul imitated the roar of a car travelling at speed, the squeal of brakes. He looked up. "The man at the gas station say thirty bucks please. I tell him I come back, pay later. What you know, he no believe me."

Another burst of laughter.

"So, I take the gun from the glove box, and pow!" Raul pointed two fingers. "I shoot up his big neon sign. Pow! Pow! And then I drive off with the tank full."

Jon eyed him cagily. "They get you on armed robbery or grand theft auto?"

"What you think, *hombre*? Those lousy pigs in LA get me on both."

Rees groaned. "Bro, I know where you are coming from. Yeah. With me, it was cars and GBH."

"GBH?" Karin asked. "What does that stand for?"

"They never did tell me."

She frowned. "They sure as hell would if you did whatever that is over here."

"All right then. It means I hit one of the cops taking me in. That's how I've ended up out here with the rest of you."

Everyone fell silent, all eyes on Karin.

She sighed. "That seems to leave only me."

"Girl, you don't have to tell nobody," Rees said.

"Honey, that wouldn't be fair." Karin lowered her head. "They called it soliciting. I guess I got into bad company."

"*Chica*, you are okay now," Raul fingered a chord on his guitar. "You are with us."

Leem took the guitar from him and started to sing Jailhouse Rock. Everyone joined in.

Through the stillness of the forest the sound of voices singing carried to a clearing a considerable distance away. A wood-fire burned at the centre, a reflection of the flames flickering on the windowpane of a log cabin that stood on the far side.

With his head bent and his face hidden Jimmy Mohawk sat squatted close to the fire, running the metal blade of his tomahawk over a flint stone, sharpening the edge. He was uttering an incantation in Apache. A large black dog that lay head up at his feet watched and listened attentively.

The dog growled. The distant voices, though barely louder than a whisper, had broken in.

Jimmy looked up, showing his face daubed with streaks of red and white. For a moment he was silent, listening. Then, with a sudden bloodcurdling yell, he leaped up and circled the fire brandishing the tomahawk.

SEVEN: DEAD MEN HANGING

Sam came to a standstill. "Take a look, lady."

Eileen was glad of a short break, keeping up with him had exhausted her. They had travelled non-stop through the night, and now the sun was high.

"Can you see them?" he asked.

She looked up at the sky. "Are you talking about the vultures, Sam?" There were two directly overhead.

"Heck, no. The critters have been following us all morning."

She shielded her eyes with her hand. They were standing on the edge of a flat yellow area bare of stunted shrubs or cactuses. A vast dip in the rocky plateau that she knew must once been a lake, or perhaps an inlet of the sea. "You mean the salt flats?"

"No, I don't have them in mind either, lady, they ain't worth the seeing." He pointed. "Take a *good* look this time."

She squinted. A thin dark-green line showed low on the horizon. Energy flowed back into her. "That must be the forest."

"Yep. A whole bunch of trees." He sighed. "Some ways to go yet. Reckon we'll rest up a while."

She turned away. "We don't have time for that."

Sam took hold of her arm. "Listen, the salt flats get mighty hot this time of day." He guided her to a shady spot. "Heck, either way we ain't gonna reach them trees before nightfall. And how you figure me to pick up any kind of trail in the dark?"

"No, I suppose not." She smiled. "That is unless you can see like a cat."

Sam sat down, removing his hat. "Guess I don't, lady." He let out a cackle. "Some folk though reckon I smell like a dog."

***

In the heart of the forest at around the same time - an hour before noon - Jon came to a standstill. A patch of sunlight showed on the ground ahead. Looking up he saw a gap in the over-arching trees where the upper branches had been torn away.

Rees halted with him. They were in the lead with the rest of the group straggling behind. "Is something wrong?"

"It feels like we are climbing again."

"Yeah, I know."

Jon frowned. "That can't be right." He pointed in a different direction, clear of the sunlit patch ahead. "If you ask me, we should be going that way. Downhill."

Rees brought out the pocket compass. "Man, that way is south-west. And we want to be heading due south. Right?" He offered the compass. "Take a look."

"Fuck that piece of shit. It's got to be downhill. Not up."

"Listen, it don't got to be either. And if we start guessing, bro, we ain't gonna get nowhere."

Rees walked on through the sunlit patch into the darkness beyond. The rest followed him, Jon falling in behind, last of all. Rees led the way in the gloom until he was dazzled by a sudden blaze of sunshine.

Raul, closest to him, kept his head down. "*Hombre, un pequeno avion!*"

Rees raised a hand above his eyes to shut out the glare and saw the wreck of a small airplane. It lay upended against a massive tree in a tangle of broken branches beyond the sunlit area, a distance away. Raul had moved ahead of him. They were the first to reach the plane. Together they cleared thick heavy branches obscuring the cockpit windshield.

The glass was intact, covered in grime. Rees rubbed a patch clear, giving him a view of the cockpit. "Shit," he muttered, backing away. There were two decaying corpses inside, the pilot and his passenger.

Raul wiped more grime from the windshield. Everyone else had stepped back a few paces, horror-struck.

Karin covered her face. "How awful."

"Poor sods." Fara shuddered and turned to Jon. "Do you think anyone knows about them?"

"It looks like we are the first ones here."

Rees shrugged. "There's nothing we can do for them, people. We'll tell the law as soon as we get to San Petro."

"Are you nuts?" Jon said. "I'm not telling the San Petro cops a fucking word about this."

Raul was listening. "You are right, *compadre. Es cierto* the pigs get us arrested for something." He looked at Leem. "It is the same where you come from, no?"

"Yeah." Leem snorted. "Over there they would get us for looting maybe."

"The Mex cops do that, too," Jon said.

"Is that what you think, *compadre?*" Raul shrugged. "Maybe we should have a look inside."

Jon frowned. "Shit, man. What the hell do you expect to find?"

"I have no idea." Raul forced his way through the branches to the cockpit door.

Karin's voice was a whisper. "Rees, we have to tell someone. Don't we?"

"I don't know, we'll have to take a vote." He gripped her hand. "All I know for sure is that you and me are done here."

The rest stayed and watched Raul heave on the cockpit door. It appeared to be jammed. He straightened. "Give me a hand, *compadre.*"

Jon picked up his backpack. "I'd just as soon leave the dead be." He looked at Fara. "Coming?"

She nodded.

Raul's gaze shifted to Leem. "Are you staying, *amigo*?"

"Yeah. I want to see what you might find inside."

"Okay." Raul placed both hands on the jammed door and leaned back. "I give it another try."

The cockpit came ajar, a gap of a few inches.

Holding his nose, Raul turned to Leem. "We go in together, yes?"

"Ugh!" Leem shuddered. "It's the stink, man. I can smell it from here."

"Okay, you can go. I'll catch you all up."

"All right, I'll tell them."

Raul waited a while to make sure Leem was out of sight before turning back to the cockpit door. This time it opened easily. Reaching inside, he unzipped the dead pilot's flying jacket, pulling the garment out of the cockpit. There was a leather cardholder in the top pocket. A pilot's license with a photo lay folded inside, in the name of Pedro Angel Mendez. His attention shifted warily from the document to the forest around him. He was alone, the quietness broken by the buzz of insects attracted by the smell of rotting flesh.

Raul un-looped the guitar from his shoulder. Squeezing his hand through the sound-hole, he unclipped a mobile phone.

***

Jason Bligh was in the Heronimo morgue when the phone call came. The sheriff had driven him there, picking him up from El Cochise, the top-ranked hotel in town. At the time he was sipping a vintage single malt in the bar. "No rush, finish your drink," Muller said, "I fancy I'll have one myself."

"A scotch?" the barman asked.

"Sure."

The barman poured a standard blend into a shot glass. The sheriff swallowed the whisky in a single gulp.

They found the morgue attendant waiting for them in a bare tiled room at the rear of the jailhouse. He sprang to his feet like a man eager to get out of there. "Go ahead, Joe," Muller said. "Roll him out."

Joe pulled open one of the large metal drawers set into the wall. Jason looked down at the corpse and nodded.

"Your man, I take it?" Muller said.

"That's right. Dan Glasson, a Californian state prison guard." At that moment, the call came, the mobile phone vibrating in Jason's pocket. He reached into his jacket. "Do you mind, sheriff?"

"Shjt, no. I guess we have seen enough of Danny-boy."

The morgue attendant rolled the drawer back into the wall.

Jason answered the call a few paces away. "You got something to tell me?"

"I'm by the plane. A two-seater with two dead guys inside."

"Are you alone?"

"Sure. I told the others I'd catch them up."

"An idea of where you are?"

"I reckon maybe twenty, twenty-five miles south of the pass."

"Is that the closest you can give me?"

"Yeah, but I'll light a fire. You should see the smoke coming up through a gap in the trees, the one made by the plane coming down."

"Don't worry. We'll find it."

Jason pocketed the phone. The sheriff was watching him. "The airplane?"

He nodded, and they both hurried out of the jailhouse.

"Your man say where the airplane is?"

"More or less."

***

Jimmy Mohawk loped across the clearing to the log cabin on the far side. He was sweating, he had run several miles through the forest. His dog had run ahead of him and was crouched on the porch, panting. "Good boy," he said and entered the cabin, leaving the door wide open behind him.

A few moments passed before he emerged from the cabin. The dog, a massive black hunting dog, bounded up, excited to see him. Jimmy was holding a mottled piece of wood in his hand and carrying a coil of thin rope over his shoulder.

The dog followed him back across the clearing into the forest.

Jimmy made his way to a sapling a few paces from the edge and threw the rope over a high overhanging branch. Both ends of the rope were within reach. He tied one end to a metal stake that had been driven deep in the ground and knotted the other end into a sliding loop. Tugging down brought the branch lower and directly above two embedded wooden stakes. Jimmy tightened the sliding loop around them and slotted in the trip wood.

A wag of the tail from the dog. The trap was set

***

Fara glimpsed Rees and Karin through the trees ahead of them. "There they are, Jon."

"Yeah, I know."

Rees waited for them. He was making his way along what appeared to be a track, knowing that the others would find him easier to follow.

"You changed direction, pal," Jon said as he drew near.

"Yeah, a few degrees east, that's all. The way I see it, this path has got to end up somewhere."

Jon took the lead, raising the pace. They came into a more open area. A massive tree had fallen a while ago, bringing down the smaller ones. All that remained was the trunk.

"Slow down, bro," Rees said. "We don't want to lose Leem and Raul."

Jon halted. "I guess not. Let's stop right here."

Leem was the first to reach them, he was breathless. "For fucks sake," he gasped, "I thought I'd never find you."

Rees frowned. "Where the hell is Raul?"

"I don't know. I ain't seen him."

"You left him by the plane on his own?" Jon asked.

"It was the smell inside. I thought I'd throw up."

"He opened the cabin door then?"

"Yeah. He said he'd catch up with us."

"All right," Rees said. "We'd better wait for him."

Jon disagreed. "Listen, nobody told the guy to fuck with that plane. I say we move on, let him catch *us* up."

Rees eyed Jon. "How come you're in such a hurry, bro?"

"Not me, man. You're the one says we should get to San Petro on time."

"A few minutes ain't gonna make a lot of difference." Rees spotted the fallen tree trunk. "Anyway, Fara and Karin could do with a rest." He pointed. "Over there looks somewhere we can sit."

Rees led the way. The wood, grey with age, had the heady aroma of old furniture stored in an attic undisturbed for years. Everyone, except Jon, sat down at the narrower end of the trunk, the two girls next to each other, their legs dangling.

Fara sighed. "What wouldn't I do for a fag."

"Tell me about it." Karin picked off pieces of decaying wood, crumbling the fragments in her fingers. "Honey, the way I feel I'd smoke this crap."

Jon raised his hand. "Hear that? Somebody is coming."

Raul appeared. He sauntered over to the two girls. "Hey, have you missed me, *chicas*?"

Karin replied. "Like a hole in the head."

He smiled at Fara. "How about you, skinny ass. You miss me?"

"You took your bloody time, Raul. We've been waiting here for ages."

He glanced at Jon. "If you had stayed to help me maybe I get here sooner."

"Did you find anything inside?" Rees asked. "Do you know who the two dead men were?"

"I have no idea. But sure, I find something." Raul opened his backpack and brought out a carton of Mexican cigarettes. "Small and dark, like me. Who wants?"

Fara stretched out for the carton eagerly. "I do."

Raul moved the cigarettes beyond her reach and turned to Karin. "How about you, big ass. You want?"

"I told you, like a hole in the head."

Raul sighed. He shrugged at Fara. "Sorry, *chica*, I think I keep them for myself."

"No, please, Raul, she didn't mean it." Fara searched for a reason. "She was concerned about you, that's why."

He looked at Karin. "Is that right? You worry for me?

She shrugged. "Yeah. A little."

"Okay." He tossed the pack of Mexican cigarettes to her.

Karin tore the carton open and gave a packet to Fara.

"What about me?" Leem asked.

Jon interrupted. "Quiet." They all listened. "You hear that?"

The sound was the clatter of a helicopter, growing louder. Nobody moved, the cigarettes forgotten. The clatter became deafening as the aircraft passed unseen overhead, hidden by the forest canopy.

Leem was the first to speak. "That could be Mr Bligh looking for us."

Karin was next. "What do we do, Rees?"

He looked hard at Jon. "I think we are doing good without him."

"That is bullshit, Rees," Leem said. "We are fucking lost."

Jon turned to him. "You are the one talking crap, pal. How do you know the chopper up there is looking *for us*?"

"It must be. There's nobody else down here."

"How about the two dead guys?"

"Well, yeah, maybe…" Leem was flustered. "But it sounded like Mr Bligh's."

"Yeah, exactly the same," Fara said.

Jon shrugged. "How can you tell? You ever heard any other one before?"

"Yeah, of course I have. On TV."

"What should we do, boss?" Raul asked.

"Use our heads. Even if it is Mr Bligh, how will he spot us down here? We've got no choice. We've got to push on."

Rees set off along the trail with Raul and Jon. Leem and the two girls lit their cigarettes before following them.

Up above, the sky was cloudless apart from a few wisps of high cirrus. A bright sunny spring day. Looking down Jason Bligh had a clear view of shifting treetops. Ahead, though, he faced a glaring blaze of sunlight. Muller was in the seat next to him, wearing sunglasses. "Do you see any sign of smoke, sheriff?"

"Not a puff."

Jason abruptly veered the helicopter they had travelled almost thirty miles beyond the mountain pass.

Muller took off his sunglasses. "Are you giving up on finding the airplane, Mr Bligh?"

"No, I'm circling back, sheriff. We'll get a better view with the sun at our back."

Soon afterwards a patch of smoke showed to starboard. He altered course in its direction. "See that, Muller?"

"Sure do. What now, Mr Bligh?"

"We go take a closer look."

He hovered over the gap in the trees, establishing their position using GPS, before heading back to Heronimo airfield.

***

The trail straightened. Rees checked the pocket compass. Raul and Jon halted with him. "We are heading due south again," he said.

Jon frowned. "Are you sure?"

"Yeah. Have a look."

"That's okay, I will take your word for it."

"Me too," Raul said. "Maybe this trail will lead us all the way to Mexico."

"Bro, it's got to lead to some place."

Leem caught up with them. "Is this a breather, Rees?"

"Not yet, we keep moving." Daylight was fading.

The trail ended at the edge of an extensive clearing. They halted a short distance away. By then dusk had fallen but through the trees a log cabin could be made out on the far side of the cleared area. It was a low structure with a sloping log roof that overhung a planked porch, the overhang supported by four wood posts, one at each corner, the other two standing outside a window and a door.

They moved back a few yards out of sight from the cabin, leaving Raul to keep watch.

"What do you make of it?" Rees asked Jon.

He grunted. "Anybody who lives way out here has got to be some kind of nut."

"Do you see anyone?"

"No, I don't, but that doesn't mean he isn't around somewhere."

Leem was listening. "Shit, Rees, let's go and find out."

"Right. It'll be you and me then, bro, knocking on his door."

"Wait, Rees." Karin's voice was low but urgent. "I have a bad feeling about this."

"Look, we ain't come to rob the place."

"I just know something bad is bound to happen."

"What can happen?" Leem asked. "It beats sleeping in a tent, don't it?"

"Dead right," Rees said. "Me and Leem will take a closer look. The rest of you stay hidden."

They returned to Raul watching the cabin through the trees. "See anyone, *compadre*?" Jon asked.

Raul shook his head. "I think nobody is there." He turned to Rees. "You want I go make sure?"

"No. Me and Leem will do that."

Karin grabbed Rees's arm, holding him back. "It doesn't need two of you."

Rees hesitated.

Raul raised a hand. "Okay, boss. I will go with him."

Leem led the way through the trees towards the edge of the clearing. "What's it like, in Mexico?"

"Good, if you know your way around."

"Jon is not your type. Take me, instead."

"I think I stick with him."

Leem halted. "Why? Don't you like me?"

"Sure, I like you, *chico*." Raul squeezed his arm. "Maybe the three of us can go there together, huh?"

Leem smiled and they both crept toward the edge of the clearing. The cabin showed through the trees. Leem took another step for a closer view. His foot landed on the trip stick lodged between the wood pegs, the cord loop tightened around his ankle, the rope jerked him upwards.

Leem screamed. He was dangling upside down from a tree branch six feet above the ground.

Raul climbed swiftly to the overhanging branch. His body weight bent the branch down as he moved along to the rope, lowering Leem. When Leem gently reached the ground, he slid down himself. Moments later Rees and Jon reached them. Together they got Leem onto his feet. He tottered.

Rees turned to Jon. "Me and Raul will bring him. Go and see if anyone is in the cabin."

"I'll come with you," Fara said.

Jon knocked on the cabin door, there had been no sound or movement from within. "Open up. We need some help."

Leem's gasp from behind broke the silence. "Jesus! You are hurting me."

Jon banged his fist on the door, raising his voice. "Hey, you hear me in there?" A hard push moved the door a crack, a pull swung it open. "Wait here," he told Fara before entering.

The room was deserted, bare of furniture apart from a chair by the window and four more chairs around a table in what was plainly the dining area. The floor was wood planked like the porch. At the centre, a chimney rose from a cast iron stove to the roof.

Beyond the dining area on the right-hand side, the room extended to form a kitchen at the rear. The walls carried a cupboard with drawers, a sink, and shelves of canned food and bottled water.

On the other side, level with the dining area, Jon saw a door set in a logged wood partition. Crossing the floor, he heard his footsteps echo on the wood planks. The cabin was raised on stilts a foot or more above the ground.

A metal bolt held the door closed. Jon slid the bolt open and entered a room that was small and windowless. It contained a single bed and a chest of drawers. There was another sliding bolt on the inside of the door. "It's okay," he called. "Fetch Leem in."

Raul and Rees edged through the door supporting Leem between them.

Jon was waiting. "Bring him over here," he said, and moved way, leaving space.

They eased Leem to the bed. He lowered himself gingerly onto the edge. Raul placed a hand on his shoulder. "How do you feel, *chico*?"

"I don't know. My leg has gone numb." leem gave a sob. "It...it's like I've only got one."

Fara went over to him. "Don't wet yourself, they are both still there." She lifted his legs onto the bed and pulled a blanket up over him. "You need to rest, that's all."

He tried to sit up. "You are all lying to me. I'll never be able to walk again."

Karin eased him back. "Stop acting stupid. Leem. Fara is right. You will be fine."

"No, you are leaving me here to die."

Rees sighed. "Girls, see what you can do for him."

Raul followed Rees into the living room closing the door behind him. Rees flattened the map out on the table. "I'm going for help."

Raul glanced at the window. "It is dark soon. How far you think you will get?"

"I'll head east for…for Vega." Rees traced his finger across the blank area of the map to a named town. "Here. On the Texas border."

Jon straightened up. He was lighting a fire in the stove. "That is tough country to cross. Day or night." He came over, his tone sombre. "Rock, desert, salt flats."

Rees folded the map. "Don't worry. I'll get there somehow."

"Hold on a minute, pal." Jon cocked his head. "Wouldn't you say Leem is the type of guy who lays it on a bit?"

Rees frowned. "Yeah, I would. But I'm not too sure he is this time."

"*Hombre*, we should wait till morning," Raul suggested. "If he is still bad, I will come with you."

"Pal, we'll both come with you," Jon added.

Rees turned, Fara had come out of the bedroom. "How is he?"

"You know Leem, Rees." Her tone was scornful. "Poor thing! Now he says he's feeling icy-cold all over."

"No problem with that." Jon gave a laugh. "There's a heap more firewood out there just waiting to be chopped up."

Raul eyed him. "*Es cierto, compadre*. Let's do this now. I will help you."

"Okay."

"Have you got something to tell me?" Jon said. They were standing by a pile of logwood at the side of the cabin.

Raul examined the large axe that lay on top of the chopping block. "Yes. The blade is sharp. No rust."

"That's handy." Jon placed a piece of log on the block. "Anything else in mind?"

Si, Mexico. What do you think?"

"Why not? It's closer than Texas."

"*Ole. Viva Mexico*." Raul swung the axe down, splitting the wood in two.

***

Warming herself by the fire, Eileen pondered whether after all Sam had the eyes of a cat. More likely, she decided, the old-timer possessed the homing instinct of a messenger pigeon.

About two hours earlier, they had been making their way, side by side, through scrub, their shadows lengthening ahead, until the moment that the last of the sun slipped below the horizon behind them, and night fell with startling suddenness.

She had lost her sense of direction, the thickening line of forest that she used as her guide had melted away into the darkness. The old-timer, however, carried on, not slowing for an instant. She followed him, not more than a pace behind.

At length she felt him grip her arm. Her response was immediate. "Sam, I am fine." She was shivering, the temperature had dropped, the heat of the desert gone, she thought that might be the reason he had taken hold of her.

He pointed. A blacker mass in the darkness had loomed up ahead. "Lady, I don't want to lose you in them there trees."

He kept hold of her, slowing when they came to the bole of a towering oak. "This is as good a spot as any," he said.

She helped him gather twigs and light a fire.

Now, warming herself, she asked, "Do you think we are ahead of them, here in the forest."

"Sure, unless they got wings."

"Or perhaps got lost somewhere on the way."

He poked at the fire. "Quit worrying about them kids. We'll track 'em down, soon as we hit their trail."

***

Karin and Fara came into the candlelit bedroom together. Leem was lying in the bed. "Sit up," Fara said.

Karin held a mug to his lips. "Here, you need something warm. It will help you to sleep."

Leem took a swallow. He grimaced and pushed the mug away. "Tomato soup. I hate the fucking stuff."

"Drink it. It will do you good."

He looked at Fara. "Ain't there nothing else to eat?"

"Not a bloody thing."

Karin put the mug to Leem's lips again. "Come on, now. You are acting like a child."

He managed a swallow, spilling a little.

"You are slobbering again," Fara said.

"That's not fair, the way I feel."

"Look, I'm sorry about what happened to you." She leaned forward and wiped his chin with her handkerchief. "But you always slobbered."

Leem sighed. "Yeah, you're dead right. I'm a mess." He gave a sob, his eyes tearful. "My whole life has been a rotten mess."

"Ah, poor me!" Karin echoed his sob. "You shouldn't be talking that way about yourself."

"It's the truth. For the first time, I can see everything clearly."

"All right," Fara said, "you made a few mistakes. Doesn't everybody?"

"Yeah. But I made them all."

Karin giggled. "Honey, surely not *all*?"

Their mood changed, they became light-hearted, swapping stories about their mistaken pasts. Leem's eyes closed. The two girls fetched their sleeping bags and stretched out on the wooden floor.

Raul, in the living room, laid his sleeping bag close to the bedroom door. From there he could hear any sound made in either room, and by raising his head he was able to make out Jon in his sleeping bag beneath the cabin window. Rees was out of sight on the kitchen floor, but his breathing had the regularity of someone deep in slumber.

Raul waited for the last glow of the stove fire to die before rising to his feet. The luminous hands of his wristwatch showed past midnight. For a while he stood there unmoving in the pitch-blackness, listening intently. Satisfied that nobody was awake, he took the mobile phone out from his guitar and tiptoed barefooted to the cabin door.

Easing the iron bolt open made a faint squeak. Once again Raul stood stock-still, listening. Neither of the sleepers stirred, their breathing remained steady. Reassured he stepped outside, closing the door noiselessly behind him.

The clearing was moonlit except where the cabin threw a shadow, Raul stayed in the shadow until he reached the forest. He went several paces deeper to ensure that he was beyond the earshot of a listener in the cabin before dialling and placing the phone to his ear. Despite that, his voice was barely above a whisper. "Did you locate the plane wreck?"

Jason answered. "No problem, your fire worked fine, we spotted the smoke a mile off." he grunted. "Cleaned out, like you said."

"Our boy didn't turn a hair."

"He will, sooner or later. Stay close to him, that's all. Any idea where you are right now?"

"Holed up in a log cabin, ten, fifteen miles south of the wreck. It's in a clearing. Big enough to see from the air. Big enough to land a chopper."

"Don't worry, I'll find it."

"Listen, one of the limeys stepped into some kind of animal trap." Raul chuckled. "Next minute, he's dangling ass-up in the air."

"Nothing serious, then."

"No. But I guess we won't be leaving for yet a while." He paused. "It will give me the time to check out the area."

"You're thinking it's where they make the drop?" Jason paused. "Okay. But take care."

Raul lowered the phone from his ear. The call had ended.

A shadowy figure rose behind him. A loop of cord drew tight around his throat. His fingers clawed at the noose in vain. His eyes bulged, his hands fluttered and became still. In less than a minute his struggle was over, his lifetime concluded.

EIGHT: CABIN FEVER

It was early morning when Eileen opened her eyes. A low shaft of sunlight through the trees had awoken her. Dazzled, she lay on her side for a while, unable to place herself until, turning her head, she remembered lying down beneath the branches and leaves of the oak tree towering above. Sam was watching her. He picked up his flask. She yawned. "Don't you ever sleep, Sam?"

"I reckon as how the older you gets, the less shut-eye you needs." He offered the flask. "I made us a brew."

The metal bottle felt icy, not warm, in her hands. "Cold tea?" she asked.

"Nope."

She unscrewed the lid. The aroma reminded her of wood smoke. "How do I know I will like this?"

"Heck, no harm in giving the brew a try."

She took another sniff. "It smells peaty, like whisky."

He cackled. "Well, one thing it ain't is whisky."

She took a sip and then a quick swallow. "Nice flavour. Your brew tastes good. What did you use?"

"Berry juice and pine nuts. A trick I learned from an old injun pal."

"He should bottle the stuff it would sell like mad." She gave him back the flask after a long swallow. "Sorry, not much left."

"No matter. I had my fill a while ago."

Gazing around the silent forest, a frown came on her face. "Where the hell do you think they are, Sam?"

"Can't say, till we pick up a trail." Sam downed the rest of the brew. "Heck, lady, we'll find them."

She sighed. "I sure hope you are right, old timer."

***

It was the sound of voices, not daylight, that woke Rees. He lay in semi-darkness on the floor of the kitchen in his sleeping bag. The voices he heard belonged to Fara and Karin. He dressed quickly.

Stepping out of the kitchen gave him a view of the living room. Daylight showed through the cabin window, morning had come. There was no sign of

Raul or Jon, their sleeping bags lay empty on the floor.

The two girls were sitting at the dining table, smoking. He went over to them. "How is Leem?"

Karin answered. "Sleeping like a baby."

"Yeah, a cry-baby," Fara added.

"No, I ain't." Leem had walked in, unseen, from the bedroom. "Got one of them fags for me?"

"Are you fit then, bro?" Rees asked.

"Of course, I am." Leem stepped towards them. "Why shouldn't I be?"

Fara lit the cigarette he took from the packet on the table. "You don't deserve one. Not after all that silly fuss you made."

"Honest, I wasn't putting it on. Anybody would have been shit-scared after what happened."

Karin sighed. "Do you mean the sudden shock, Leem?"

"Yeah, exactly."

"Oh dear. Sometimes it does odd things to people." She frowned and peered at him. "Hey, Leem. Are you losing hair?"

He ran his fingers up through his scalp. "Shit, have either of you two got a mirror." Both girls laughed. "Hey, that ain't funny."

"No, but *you* are, blood." Rees gestured around the room. "Where are the others, Karin?"

She glanced at Fara. "Are you talking about Jon and Raul?"

Rees grunted. "Yeah. Those two, who else would I mean?"

He saw her glance at Fara again.

The girl from Liverpool lowered her eyes. "We don't know, we haven't seen either of them."

His gaze shifted back to Karin. "Have you got any idea where they might be?"

Karin sighed. "Rees, we were wondering if..."

Fara interrupted her. "*You* were, not me."

"Okay." Karin turned back to Rees. "Look, I was wondering if maybe they had made their break for Mexico, like they kept saying they would."

Rees scowled. "Stay here, all three of you."

A few strides took him out on to the porch, the cabin door had been left unbolted. For a moment he stood there with one hand on the support post, his gaze sweeping the clearing and the forest edge. A creak from above made him back a few paces off the porch onto the clearing. Looking up, he saw Jon on his stomach slithering down the overhanging roof. He watched him drop down to the wood planks. "What were you doing up there?" he asked.

Jon turned to face him. "I was looking out for Raul."

Rees noticed the axe in his hand. "What the fuck is going on?"

"Raul hasn't come back. Not since last night."

"How do you know that? Did you see him leave?"

"Yeah, I did. I got up and watched him through the window. The noise he made opening the door bolt woke me up."

"Maybe he has pissed off to Mexico."

"No way. We aimed to make it there together. The guy would have told me."

"You've got a lot of faith in him, bro."

"Yeah, I do. He left his guitar behind." Jon shouldered the axe. "Let's go take a look around."

Rees followed him across the clearing. Jon stopped at the edge by a bushy shrub. "The last I saw of him was here."

"Well, he ain't here now," Rees said, and stepped past him into the forest. A few paces in, a glitter caught his eye. "What is that?"

A step closer revealed a mobile phone lying in the undergrowth. He stooped. A swishing sound made him straighten.

Raul was hurtling head-first towards him.

Rees ducked. The corpse of Raul swung back and forth, dangling from a rope tied to a tree branch.

***

Entering the cabin, Jon saw Leem and the two girls sitting around the dining table. They were smoking, the air heavy with the sweet aroma of Mexican cigarettes. Fara's gasp showed relief at seeing him. "Jon, we missed you. Where have you been?"

"Nowhere in particular," he responded, keeping his tone casual.

"Anyway, I'm real glad you are back," Karin said. "I thought you and Raul might have lit out on us."

"It seems you were wrong." Jon rolled up his sleeping bag. "Get packed. We are leaving."

Leem frowned. "Oh yeah? Since when are *you* giving us orders?"

"I'm not. If you want to stick around, that's up to you."

"Is that what Rees told you, we are leaving?" Karin wanted to know.

"Yeah." Jon fastened his backpack. "He's waiting outside. He asked for you to bring his stuff, along with your own."

Coming out of the cabin, Jon pushed the door closed behind him. "Rees," he called, his voice not loud enough to be heard inside.

Rees was crouched on the roof, gripping the axe. He jumped down. "How did they take it, bro?"

"I didn't tell them about Raul." Jon turned to face the clearing, "Have you spotted anyone?"

"No. Nothing."

"Listen, I am going to take another look at him."

"Shit man, Raul is dead. He won't be no help."

"There is something I'd like to check out. You don't have to wait for me, pal. I'll be following after."

"All right." Rees shrugged and gave him the axe. "You may need this, bro."

"Don't worry. We'll meet up later."

Rees's eyes stayed on Jon. He watched him cross the clearing to the shrub where they had entered the forest not long ago. A moment after Jon disappeared from view amongst the trees, he heard Leem and the two girls come out of the cabin. Karin had brought his backpack, his sleeping bag neatly rolled. "Thanks," he said. "Are we all set?"

"Wait." Fara frowned. "Where is Jon?"

"Jon is good, he'll catch us up. Right. Let's get moving."

"What about Raul, then," Leem said. "Aren't we going to wait for him?"

"Raul won't be coming."

"Why not?"

"We haven't got time for that now. Let's go."

"Where is he? I want to know." Leem took off his backpack. "Listen, I'm not leaving here until I know."

"Shit man, you won't want to hear this." Rees sighed. "Raul won't be coming because he is dead."

The girls looked at Rees in horror.

Leem laughed nervously. "You are just saying that to scare us."

"Yeah, you are right, all of us should be scared. That's why we are leaving. Somebody murdered him."

Fara's eyes widened. "Rees, who would do that?"

"I've got no idea who he was or why he did it. And I ain't hanging around to find out." He turned away from the cabin.

An arrow whistled past him, thudding into the cabin door.

He ducked low. "Get down! All of you."

They crouched, cowering.

A second arrow thudded into the wooden porch support.

It was a cue for Rees to act. "Back inside! Everyone."

They scuttled into the log cabin, Rees entering last of all. He stayed by the door, peering out. Leem had gone over to the window. "Can you see him from there?" Rees asked.

"No, no one."

"He'll be in the trees, opposite. That's where the second arrow came from."

"Yeah, I'm looking."

Karin took a cigarette from the packet on the table. The cigarettes and the lighter had been left behind by Fara in the rush to leave. "Gee, I need a smoke. How about you?"

Fara shook her head.

"Are you sure?"

"Not me. I couldn't."

"Honey, mind if I borrow your lighter?" Karin lit the cigarette, not waiting for an answer. She grunted. "I never liked Raul anyway, he had a dirty little mind."

Fara nodded. "Yeah, really dirty. I heard him talking that way to you."

"No, you never," Leem blurted.

Rees glanced at Leem. He was frowning at the two girls. "See anything?"

"No." Leem sneaked a look through the window. "Not a thing."

"Me, neither, but keep watching." Rees bolted the door and went over to the girls.

Karin looked up at him. "What are we going to do?"

"I don't know but we'll come up with something." He called to Leem, still at the window. "Any ideas, bro?"

"Yeah, I've got one." Leem came over to the table. "What if it was Jon who killed Raul. And now he's trying to kill us."

Fara gave a weary sigh. "Leem, I always knew you were plain daft." She looked at Rees. "He is talking nonsense, Rees. As usual."

Rees frowned. "I ain't so sure."

Fara's eyes blazed. "Fuck both of you! Jon wouldn't kill anybody." She took a cigarette from the pack. "He...he is too nice."

Leem snorted. "Is that why the guards had him handcuffed. Because he was too nice?"

She lit the cigarette. "I didn't ask them."

"Well, I'll keep looking," Leem said and went back to the window.

Karin squeezed Fara's hand. "Honey don't get too stuck on a man. Jon is cool but the guy is a pusher, that's about all we know for sure about him."

"Quiet!" Leem hissed. "He's outside."

Rees moved silently to the cabin door.

Leem came over. "Are we letting him in?"

"Yeah, but I ain't taking no chances."

Rees waited until there was a knock on the door. He nodded, and Leem slid back the bolt.

The door swung open, and Jon stepped in, holding the axe. He was taken by surprise, Rees pinned him from behind and Leem grabbed the axe. "What the hell are you at?"

Rees forced him into a chair at the table. "Don't move," he said and went back to bolt the door.

Jon turned to Fara, Leem was standing over him with the axe. "What is this all about?"

"They are saying you killed Raul."

Jon raised his voice. "Is that what you think, boss?"

Leem answered. "Yeah, you're a psycho, that's why," he said. "You want to kill all of us."

"I wasn't talking to you, asshole." He looked at Rees. "Well?"

Rees sat down opposite him at the table. "First I want to know what the fuck you have been doing out there."

"Like I told you, checking up on Raul." Jon reached into his pocket. "I found this on him. It explains why he was snooping around the plane wreck." He handed the pilot's license to Rees.

Rees frowned and passed the license to Leem. "Is that why Raul was on this hike?"

"I guess the guy who killed him thought so."

"What guy?" Leem tossed the license onto the table in disgust. "Rees, he's just giving us a load of bollocks."

"I ain't so sure. How do we know Raul wasn't a snoop?" Rees narrowed his eyes at Jon. "Are you saying he was a copper?"

"Yeah, I am." Jon gave a shrug. "Why would they use a guy who wasn't one of their own?"

"Wow, a cop who talked dirty." Karin raised her hands as if in shock. "He sure had me fooled."

Fara gave a rueful laugh. "The sod had us all going."

Leem frowned at them, bewildered. "I don't get it." His eyes shifted to Jon. "Why send a cop with *us*? How could they be sure we'd find the fucked-up airplane?"

"Sorry, pal. I didn't get round to asking him."

Rees raised his hand. "Shh." A creak came from above. "You hear that?"

The creaking continued. Everyone listened transfixed.

"He is on the roof." Rees's voice was low, a whisper. He crept to the door and gently eased back the bolt. Jon and Leem were with him. He pulled open the door. His eyes widened. "Shit!" He ducked back.

Karin screamed.

The body of Raul swung in the doorway.

"Son of a bitch." Jon muttered.

Fara saw him bunch his fists and move forward. "Jon, don't go out there..."

Her warning came too late. There was a whoosh. Jon staggered back with an arrow protruding from his shoulder. She and Karin helped him away.

Rees bolted the door. "Don't move from that window, Leem. If you see him, give me a yell."

Rees went over to the table, the girls had Jon seated in one of the chairs. Fara was trying to take off his jacket. He winced. The jacket was pinned by the arrow.

We'll have to cut around it," Rees said. He found a large pair of scissors in the cutlery drawer.

Fara held out her hand. "I'll do i." She used the scissors to cut the arrow shaft in two where it protruded and then eased the sheepskin jacket off Jon. The arrowhead was buried in his flesh. "Jon, we have to get the rest out."

"Yeah, but how will you do that? It's kind of deep."

"There is only one way."

"I guess so." He stiffened. "Go ahead."

"Try not to move." She looked at Karin, standing behind the chair. "Hold him still, will you?"

Karin locked her arms around Jon.

Fara gripped the projecting piece of shaft and pushed hard. The arrowhead emerged and slid to the floor. She staunched the blood flow with her handkerchief. "It's all right. The hankie is clean."

"You were great," Jon murmured. "You should be a nurse."

Fara fought back her tears. She leaned forward and kissed him on the mouth.

Karin laughed. "I bet they don't teach that in nursing school."

***

At midmorning Jon crossed the cabin to the window. The girls had finished with him. They had bandaged his shoulder, using their handkerchiefs washed and dried by the stove fire. Last of all, Fara stitched the hole in his jacket.

Leem and Rees were standing by the window. "Any sign of the son of a bitch, pal?"

Rees grunted. "You'd know if we had."

Yeah, I guess I would. Nothing so far."

"Maybe he's lost interest in us," Leem suggested.

Rees shook his head. "Psychos don't work that way. They never give up on who they are after."

Leem sighed. "What are we going to do, then? Nobody even knows that
we are here."

"You're forgetting whoever it was who set up Raul on this trip. He'll know where we are." Rees looked hard at Jon. "Any idea who he might be?"

"Your guess is as good as mine."

Rees gave a shrug. "It don't matter anyway. Whoever he is, he'll want to know why Raul ain't telling him what's going on."

Leem frowned. "Are you saying Raul had a mobile phone?"

"Yeah. That is exactly what I am saying."

The day had reached late afternoon when they pushed open the cabin door. They had waited until the sun had sunk low over the forest, casting long shadows across the clearing to the far edge. The dining table stood on its end in the cabin doorway, the top facing outwards. Crouching behind, Rees,

Leem and Jon manoeuvred the table through the doorway, past the hanging corpse of Raul, and on to its side.

Rees raised his head. An arrow thudded into the tabletop, making him duck down. "He is in the trees, over to the right. Are you two ready?"

They nodded.

All right. Keep him occupied."

Jon reached up as if to untie Raul. An instant later an arrow swished into the wooden support post. Beyond him, Rees was belly-sliding on the porch towards the end of the cabin.

Unnoticed by the others, Karin crept through the doorway and followed him.

Leem lifted his head momentarily, and an arrow thwacked into Raul's corpse. By then Rees was out of sight, on his feet making his way silently along the side wall. He frowned at Karin when they reached the rear of the cabin. "What are you at, girl?"

I'm coming along. I thought you could do with some help."

Rees hesitated until he noticed the large pair of scissors in her pocket. "Yeah, I might need some. But stay close."

He tracked quickly through the darkening forest until he came to a loop of rope trailing from the overhanging branch of a tree. "This is where I spotted the phone," he whispered. "Start looking."

They circled around in the gloom, apart from each other, peering into the undergrowth. Karin halted, her eyes were sharp, her voice a hiss. "Rees!"

He went over to her. She was standing a pace away from a wide deeply dug pit. The mobile phone lay at the bottom in the middle. "Good girl."

"Wait. It looks to me like a...I don't know...like an animal trap?"

"Yeah, it does. But right now, the psycho ain't here to trap us, is he?"

"No, I guess not."

Kneeling, she watched him lower himself into the pit, it was more than head high. A growl made her look up. A huge black dog was crouched at the edge, its yellow eyes fixed on Rees. She tried to warn him. "Hurry up, Rees!"

He stooped to pick up the phone before starting to climb out. The dog leaped forward, knocking him back into the pit. She stood frozen to the spot.

The dog was on top of Rees, its open jaws closing on his throat.

He gasped. "Girl, I can't hold him."

Her response was instinctive. She dropped down on the dog, plunging the scissors into the animal's neck. The yellow eyes dulled, the spark of life lost, the body twitched and lay still.

Rees pushed the dead creature aside. He climbed out of the pit and reached down for her.

Standing beside him, she gave a laugh that was more like a sob. "Happy that I came then?"

He kissed her. "Yeah, over the moon."

Leem and Jon were waiting for them behind the table, the last of daylight almost gone. "Any luck?" Jon asked.

"Yeah. We found the phone." Rees took hold of a table leg. "Let's get this back inside first."

Karin ducked into the cabin. Fara took hold of her hand. "You are cool, sweetie." Together they watched the boys drag the table into the cabin.

Rees waited for Jon to slide the door bolt into place. He handed the phone to Karin. "Do you know how to call the cops?"

"You bet I do." She dialled the number and put the phone to her ear. The rest watched her. She shook her head. "Nothing."

Rees frowned. "Try again."

Karin re-dialled the number. She listened and shook her head once more.

Leem held out his hand. "Give it here. I know how they work." He opened the back of the phone. "No fucking battery."

A howl of anguish came from the forest.

Leem hurled the phone at the cabin door. "Shut up, you maniac!"

The howling continued.

Jon went to the window. "It seems like he is real upset. Any idea why?"

Karin looked tearfully at Rees. He placed his arm around her. "Yeah, it's his dog. We killed the shitty beast."

"That explains it." Jon grunted. "I guess we hang around for his next move."

Rees agreed. "Yeah, that's all we can do, watch and listen. We'll take it in turn at the window."

Leem was keeping watch when Jon got up from the table and went over to him. The anguished howling had ended earlier as abruptly as it had begun. He peered through the glass pane. Night had come, it was pitch-black outside.

"What is it?" Leem said.

"I thought I heard someone. I must be getting a little jumpy".

"We all are."

Jon went back to the table where the others were sitting. Fara squeezed his hand. "It gets you down, all this waiting."

"Why don't you and Karin grab some shuteye?"

"Yeah, it don't need all of us sitting around here," Rees said.

"No, I am not sleepy."

Karin stifled a yawn. "Well, I could sure do with some." She got to her feet, placing a hand on Rees's shoulder. "Wake me whenever, honey?"

Rees nodded, and Karin kissed him.

The bedroom door closed behind her. Fara looked at Jon, and they both giggled.

Rees frowned at them. "Look, it was her who killed the dog. She saved my life out there."

Fara cocked her head. "Is that all she did for you?"

"Shit, ain't that enough, girl?"

Fara looked at Jon, and they giggled again.

Rees got to his feet. "Cut it out, will you! I'm trying to listen." He strode over to the window. "Anyway, you two got nothing to take the piss about."

"I guess not," Jon said.

"What are you getting at?" Leem looked at each of them in turn with a puzzled expression. "What's going on around here?"

All three laughed.

"What? Tell me, Fara."

"It's nothing."

"Then why are you all laughing?"

"Because you are so funny, Leem."

He pulled a face.

They all laughed, but louder, unaware that they were overheard.

Jimmy Mohawk was creeping across the clearing, a shadow in the darkness, his foot-steps soundless in moccasins The laughter made him freeze, but only for an instant. He had a clear view of the window, and no face showed there, peering through, watching.

He made his way along the side wall to the rear of the cabin. A tangle of branches and twigs lay two paces back from the bedroom wall. Crouching he removed them, exposing the opening of a tunnel wide enough for him to squeeze through.

His ears had picked out the murmur of conversation from within, too faint for him to catch the words. Now he moved cautiously along the cabin's rear to the far side wall, squatting down where he could hear the speakers distinctly. They were sitting at the dining table.

At length, two hours at most, the bedroom door opened, and Karin came out. She stretched, reaching up. Rees was by the window. The moon had appeared above the treetops, casting the clearing in silvery light. She gave him a smile and then sat with the others at the table. "Hi."

"Did you sleep well?" Jon asked her.

"Yeah, like a baby." She looked at Fara. "Why don't you get some?"

Fara yawned. "Yeah, I think I will." She turned to Jon. "Wake me in a couple of hours, will you?"

"Okay. Two hours."

She kissed him. "Make it sooner if you need me."

Leem watched the bedroom door close behind her. "Oh. Now I see."

"See what, Leem?" Karin asked, innocently

Leem grinned. "If you don't know, I ain't saying."

Karin fluttered her eyes at Jon. "Can *you* tell me what he isn't saying?"

Jon considered the matter with a straight face. "It seems to me Leem here has got himself kind of tongue-tied. I guess he could use some help explaining."

Rees sat down at the table. "What has Leem been telling you, Karin?"

"Not a darn thing."

"That's all right then." Rees put an arm around Leem. "You see, this dude has got one dirty little mind. Ain't that right, Leem?"

"Man, sometimes I even shock myself."

"You are putting her on," Jon said.

"No, he's not." Rees tightened his hold on Leem. "Go on. Say something really bad to her."

"Do you think I should?"

Rees's nod was grave.

Leem stared fiercely at Karin. "Pink nipples."

All three boys laughed.

Karin got to her feet. "Very funny."

Rees looked up at her. "Where are you going?"

"To smoke a cigarette. That is something grown-ups do."

She disappeared into the bedroom. The boys shrugged at each other. A moment later they heard her call out. "Jon!"

He found Karin standing alone in the bedroom. The bed had been shifted, exposing the tunnel under the wall.

"What's going on?" Rees was standing in the doorway.

Jon pushed past him and unbolted the cabin door. "He has taken Fara."

"How?"

Jon left without answering.

Rees headed for the cabin door, passing by Leem. "Don't leave. Stay here with Karin."

Rees came out of the cabin at a run. The clearing showed empty in the moonlight. Jon had halted at the centre, listening. "Hear anything?" he asked.

Jon shook his head.

"They can't have got far."

A rustling sound.

Rees pointed. "It came from over there."

They ran across the clearing and plunged into the darkness of the forest. "Quiet!" Rees whispered. A moment of silence. Rees raised his voice to a shout. "Fara. Can you hear me?"

A muffled gasp.

Jon turned and pushed through the hanging foliage and thick undergrowth. "This way."

Another gasp, but louder.

Jon hurried forward. The undergrowth thinned and he caught sight of Fara. She was tied around a tree, blindfolded by a handkerchief, another handkerchief stuffed in her mouth.

***

Leem stayed for a while by the window with Karin, the axe in his hand. She was sobbing. "Poor Fara!"

"Don't worry, Rees will find her."

"Alive?"

"I don't know." He turned away and bolted the cabin door. "Stay here."

"Where are you going?"

"The bedroom."

Karin held him back. "Leem. Are you sure you want to go in there?"

"It's all right. I've got this" He raised the axe above his head.

Karin followed him nervously to the bedroom door. He opened it wide. From the doorway she saw him walk over to the opening by the rear wall. "A tunnel. That's how he got in."

"Leem, come out. We can bolt the bedroom door."

"No, I'd better stay right here." He sat down on the edge of the bed with his eyes fixed on the tunnel opening. "Just in case."

She shivered. "Yes, I guess so."

"Keep watch by the window. Give me a shout when you see them."

Karin lit a cigarette at the table before going to the window. Peering through she saw Jon, Rees and Fara coming across the clearing towards her. "Leem, I can see them."

There was no answer from Leem.

Karin unbolted the cabin door: The first one through was Fara. She hugged her. "Are you okay, honey?"

"Fara is fine," Jon said.

"Did...did you see him?"

"No. He covered my eyes I couldn't see a thing."

"Where is Leem?" Rees asked.

"In the bedroom" Karin called him again. "Leem, they are here. Come on out." There was no reply. "I'll go get him."

Jon stiffened. The bedroom door was closed. He took her arm. "Hold it. Was it you who shut that door?"

"No. Leem must have."

"Why in hell would he do that?"

Karin's voice sank to a whisper. "What...what are you getting at?"

Jon eyed Rees. "Me and Rees will go fetch him."

Rees pushed open the bedroom door. Leem was sitting hunched on the bed with his back to them. "Shit bro, why don't you answer?"

Rees placed a hand on his shoulder. Leem sagged back. Karin, standing in the doorway, screamed. Leem's headless corpse lay sprawled on the bed.

NINE: CARDS ON THE TABLE

At a little after dawn Rees came out of the bedroom. Fara and Karin watched him from the dining table, they had spent most of the night there. He bolted the bedroom door and tossed the carton of cigarettes onto the table. Two packets of twenty were inside.

"Is that the last of them, Rees?" Karin asked.

"Yeah, one pack each."

Jon was standing by the window, looking out. Rees went over to him. "It's my watch now, bro. Take a break."

"To do what? Sit at the table and talk?" Jon straightened up. "Waiting for him won't get us out of here."

"You are right. But neither would walking out through that door. He's a dead shot. He'd hit you with another arrow before you took another step." Rees sighed. "Yeah, we're stuck here waiting for him. Unless he leaves us be. Or you come up with a better idea."

"I have one," Jon said. "I'll go out and talk to him."

"What makes you think he will listen?"

"It's worth a try, wouldn't you say?"

Rees glanced across at the two girls, they were listening. He gave a shrug.

Fara gripped Karin's arm, her voice an urgent whisper. "He'll end up like...like the others, Karin. Tell him."

Karin raised her voice. "Rees is right, Jon. The crazy son of a bitch will kill you."

"No, he won't."

Rees stepped between Jon and the cabin door. "Bro, how can you be certain he'll talk?"

"Stay out of it, pal."

"You're way ahead of us. You have been from the start. AIn't that right?" Rees saw Jon's eyes flicker. "We're in this fix together. Aren't we?"

"No, we are not. It's me he wants."

"Blood, you got some explaining to do. And you're not going nowhere till you do."

Jon sighed. "I guess not. I kind of wish we'd had this conversation sooner. Okay. Here's my story." His eyes changed their focus, as if looking into the distance. "A few months back, in San Petro, I got into a bad scene. The Mex cops dumped me at the border. Seemed like a good deal. It was that or another thirty days in a cell. Shit, I should have stayed in the slammer. It was midwinter out there."

"I'm guessing you found the airplane," Rees said.

Yeah, exactly the way you all saw it, except there was snow and ice around at the time. Nose down by a tree, the pilot and passenger hanging in their straps, the two of them both dead."

Rees grunted. "You ain't told us yet what else was in that plane."

"Nothing. I was turning away. I'd given up looking."

"What were you looking for?" Karin asked.

"Something to eat. I was starving. There was a suitcase lying in a patch of snow a few paces away. I opened it and what I found inside made me forget I was hungry."

Fara's eyes widened. "Heroin?"

No, coke. Rows and rows of cellophane bags of the stuff packed tight. Guess I wasn't gonna leave that big leather suitcase lying around for someone else to find."

Karin frowned. "You hid the coke?"

"Yeah. The whole suitcase full."

Rees narrowed his eyes. "All of it?"

"No, not all. I kept one bag."

"Anybody see you?"

"Not then, later." Jon threw a glance behind him. "I looked back when I got to the pass. There was snow all the way down to the forest. Someone was following my track up the mountainside. No way of telling if he was after me. And I sure wasn't gonna hang around to find out."

"Is that the last you saw of him?"

"No, he kept coming. Close enough for me to see he was carrying a rifle. Darn near caught me, too." Jon wiped his brow. "I got plain lucky. A guy picked me up at the roadside, took me all the way to LA."

"I don't get it," Karin said. "How did you end up here, with us?"

"The cops arrested me for selling that bag of coke."

Rees took a step closer. "Are you saying they thought you'd lead them to where you hid the rest?"

Jon's eyes re-focused. "Yeah. That is what I am saying."

Fara came over to him. "Are you going to tell *us* where, Jon?"

"I don't plan to." He explained. "Listen, it's safer for all of you if I am the only one who knows."

Rees went over to the window and peered out. "You mean we've been set up like this for a load of shit."

Jon sighed. "Look, I am real sorry. Especially about Leem."

"You are not to blame, Jon." Fara touched his arm. "How could anyone expect anything so awful to happen?"

"That isn't the truth of it. I should have known the creep would never give up on me. The fault is mine, babe." Jon's gaze shifted from her. "Rees, if he gets the coke, he leaves us be. Right?"

"You think he's the man who was chasing you with a rifle?"

"Yeah, I do."

"Then why ain't he using it?"

"I don't know. Maybe because shooting someone is noisy, I guess."

"I'm not that sure the crazy wouldn't just as soon kill us for fun."

"Look, San Petro isn't far. Two days at most. You'll have a head start on him."

"No way, bro. We set out together. And that is how we are gonna finish."

Jon's gaze shifted to the two girls. "What about them? Haven't they got a say in this?"

"You want we should put it to a vote?"

"Yeah. But in private. They might not want me to hear what they say."

Rees walked over to the table. The girls followed him. He kept his voice low. "Karin?"

"We stick together," she whispered.

Rees looked at Fara. She nodded. He turned to face Jon and saw him unbolt the cabin door. "Hold it. They want you to stay."

"My call, not theirs." Jon opened the door. "It's me," he yelled through the doorway before stepping out. "The guy you are after."

Fara moved to follow him, but Rees held her back. She struggled to free herself. "Let go of me."

"Not a chance." Gripping Fara with one arm, Rees bolted the door. "Now, listen." He released her. "We are going to play this the way your man called it."

Fara slumped at the table and buried her face in her hands. Karin put a comforting arm around her.

***

Coming out of the cabin, Jon stepped over Raul's body. His corpse had fallen overnight and lay face up by the door. For a while Jon stayed unmoving on the porch, his hand resting on the roof support post, with only his gaze shifting and searching. Nobody had answered his call. Glints of sunlight through the trees dazzled him when they caught his eye. The clearing, still darkened by overnight dampness, was deserted with no discernible movement at the forest edge – and yet he knew that someone was watching him.

Before leaving, he dragged Raul's corpse along the porch a few paces away from the door, turning him face down. It seemed the decent thing to do.

Jon entered the forest where they had found Raul hanging from a tree branch. He followed Rees's footsteps further, his purpose to make the watcher show himself. He soon came upon the animal trap. It was empty, but a mound of earth nearby, topped by a leather collar, marked the dog's grave. A quick glance around showed no sign of anyone – but he sensed again that he was being watched.

He went deeper into the forest, between the trees, his ears alert for any sound. He kept his pace unhurried and made his direction seem aimless, resisting the temptation to turn suddenly. Sooner or later the man following him would show his hand.

A sound made him come to a standstill: the clunk of a piece of wood hitting a tree trunk ahead of him. "I know you are behind me," he said aloud.

He paused to listen but heard no response.

"Here's the deal," he continued. "I take you to the coke, and you let the others go free. Agreed?"

Again, there was no reply.

Jon raised his voice. "Listen good, you creep. If you don't play along, I won't be taking you anywhere."

Heavy breathing made him turn. A man stood a pace away, his face daubed in warpaint, his hand gripping a tomahawk. A memory flashed into his mind. The man had served him lunch in the Red Eagle diner. In that same instant Jimmy grinned and swung the tomahawk down.

***

At length Rees decided that he had waited long enough, the sun was dappling the clearing golden with its rays. He turned away from the window, the axe grasped in his hand. "It's time I was going."

"Take care, Rees," Karin said.

Fara sniffed tearfully. "Are you sure you can find him?"

He had explained his plan earlier, but he repeated himself. "Don't worry, I know where Jon is headed." He looked at Karin. "Are you all right with this?"

The girl hugged him. "We will be fine." She unbolted the cabin door for him. "See you back here with Jon."

"Yeah," he said, and left her standing in the doorway.

He crossed the clearing to the spot at the far end where they had first seen the log cabin. They had numbered six then, now they were only four.

He looked back. The cabin door had been closed and the window dazzled him, a blaze of reflected sunshine, but in his mind's eye he pictured the two girls together, there behind the glass pane watching him, their arms around each other. He waved at the window and then stepped out of the sunlight into the shadowiness of the forest.

His eyes adjusted to the change rapidly, he was able to pick out the route he had followed, a path trodden by creatures of the forest and used by the man who lived in the log cabin. It would lead him to the hollow tree trunk on which the two girls had sat, and in which, he had no doubt, the cocaine lay. From Jon's account, the suitcase was too heavy to carry any further from the airplane.

There was still a distance to go when a shuffling sound came from behind that he took to be a deer or some other large creature. He turned but his view was shut off by the forest trees. He quickened his pace until, on entering a small glade, an open space of thick undergrowth, he caught the sound again, as if the creature was trailing him. He hid behind a tree on the edge and waited.

A few moments later Jon stumbled into view. His face was bloody, his hands tied in front of him.

Rees stepped forward, away from the tree, showing himself. Their eyes met. Jon stumbled again, this time deliberately. He took this to be a signal and ducked down into the undergrowth.

A voice made him raise his head. "Get up on your feet, boy."

Jon had fallen to the ground. A man was standing over him.

"That isn't easy," Jon answered. "Tied up like this."

"How about like this, then?" The man kicked him hard. He was bare-chested, wearing Levis and moccasins, his face streaked with paint, a small axe and a hunting knife at his belt

Jon struggled on to his knees.

The man heaved him up the rest of the way. "Now keep moving. I am losing patience."

Jon moved forward. "Stay cool, man. We are getting close, nearly there."

Rees watched the man fall in close behind Jon. Despite the warpaint, his face seemed familiar. All at once a name came back to him. Jimmy Mohawk, the owner of the Heronimo airfield diner.

***

The flap of birds wheeling over the treetops caught their attention. They both looked up. Sam raised his hand to his ear. "Something is scaring the critters."

They listened, scarcely breathing.

The noise of flapping wings died away, replaced by the faint drone of an approaching aircraft. The drone became a deafening clatter. They stared up at the dense canopy of the trees and saw the dark shadow of a helicopter flash by overhead.

Sam grunted. "Ain't never seen one of them birds afore in these parts."

They were sitting side by side, their backs against an oak, a break from the search for a trail. "Sam, I'm sure it's ours. The one we came in."

"Seems like we ain't the only ones hunting down them kids." He picked up his hat. "Could be that smart young feller's drawn a bead on them."

Eileen put her boots on and followed him into the forest. He took the direction the helicopter had taken.

***

Fara was the first of them to hear the far-off sound. She was sitting in a chair by the table listening to Karin, bent over Raul's guitar, sing *On Top of Old Smokey,* her voice low. She got up from the chair abruptly and went over to the window. "Karin. Quiet a moment."

Karin stopped playing and singing.

"Do you hear that?" Fara asked.

In the silence that fell in the cabin, Karin caught a sound that was no louder than the flight of a honeybee. She laid the guitar down carefully before hurrying over to Fara at the window.

The faint drone became a clatter.

All at once a helicopter came into view hovering above them. Karin turned for the door. "Come on. Let's get out there."

Fara grabbed her arm. "Hold on. I think we should wait, see who is inside."

"Don't be silly." Karin shook herself free. "Honey, if we don't show ourselves right soon, that chopper will be gone." She unbolted the cabin door. "Are you coming?"

"What for? It's landing."

Karin returned to the window. The helicopter was almost stationary, a few feet above the clearing.

"Gee, it's big. Is that the one we came in?"

"Yeah. It's the same one all right."

They watched the helicopter settle at the far edge of the clearing. Karin frowned. "Honey, tell me something. If that's the one we came in, why aren't we showing ourselves?"

"Karin, I've been doing some thinking." Fara's voice was edged with doubt. "How do we know if it's come here for us?"

"I don't follow you. What other reason can there be?" Karin's eyes widened. "Do you mean the coke?"

Fara nodded.

Karin looked hard at her. "Are you saying Mr Bligh might be the man behind all of this?"

Fara gave another nod.

Standing at the window, they saw Jason and Muller climb out of the helicopter. The pair headed across the clearing towards the log cabin.

Halfway there, Jason caught sight of a body, face down, on the porch. "Cover me, will you, Muller."

Keeping low, he ran forward to the corpse and turned it face up. "Shit! The dead guy is my man."

Muller made no response. He carried on to the cabin door, entering the room revolver in hand. Two girls were sitting at the table, smoking, one blonde, the other a redhead. He remembered seeing them in Jimmy Mohawk's diner. "Anybody else here?"

The two of them shook their heads.

His eyes shifted to the other door. "How about in there?" The girls looked at each other. He saw the blonde girl shudder. "I guess I'll go take a peek."

Fara and Karin watched him unbolt the bedroom door, saw it close behind him, unaware that Jason had come into the cabin. "What the hell has been going on?" he asked.

The two girls turned to face him but neither made any response.

"Speak up," Jason demanded. "We have a dead guy lying out there." The bedroom door opened, and he saw Muller emerge, gun in hand. "My people aren't going to like this. It's a mess."

The sheriff grunted "Well, they ain't about to get any happier." He jerked his head at the door. "We got ourselves another dead one back there."

"My god! Who?"

"That is kind of difficult to say."

Jason strode past him into the bedroom.

Fara uttered a sob. "Hs name is Leem, sheriff."

"What's been going on then, gals?"

Karin saw Jason emerge from the bedroom. "Why not ask *him*? He's the one who set it all up."

"Is that so?" Muller swung the revolver at Jason. "It seems to me, Mr Bligh, this here could be a good time for you to lay your cards on the table."

Jason lit a cigarette, inhaling deeply.

***

Rees waited for them hidden in the reedy undergrowth. The large hollow tree trunk lay in view a dozen paces away. The snap of a twig trodden underfoot made him crouch lower, grip the axe more tightly. After a few seconds he raised his head a little, aware that they had arrived. He saw Jon halt.

Jimmy shoved him forward. "Keep moving."

"Lay off, will you. This is the place I hid the stuff."

"Yeah? Where?"

"See the big dead log? That is where. Unless some other ass-hole has taken it."

Jimmy scowled. "If the coke ain't there, it's because you never put it there." He pushed Jon. "Show me."

Jon limped over to the narrower end of the fallen tree. "The trunk is hollow. I shoved the suitcase way inside." He raised his wrists. "You want I should reach in and get it?"

Jimmy pulled the hunting knife from its belt. "Yeah, sure as hell you will get it if the stash ain't there." He stabbed the knife into the tree trunk. "Afterwards, just as soon as we are done here." He took hold of Jon and threw him to the ground. "Now you stay good and still, where I can see you."

Jimmy crouched at the end of the fallen tree. He reached an arm into the hollow trunk.

Jon sat up. Beyond the tree, he saw Rees rise from the undergrowth. "Jimmy, I sure hope no rattler is curled up inside there, sleeping. They get awful annoyed if you wake them."

"Shut up! I said to stay good and still." Jimmy knelt and reached further into the trunk. He got to his feet empty-handed. "You've been lying to me, boy."

"Shit, now I remember. The case was too big to go in there. I stuffed it in the other end."

Jimmy aimed a kick at Jon. "It had better be."

Jon waited until he saw him kneel at the wide end of the trunk. "Like I said, watch out for any rattler asleep in there."

Rees, axe in hand, moved silently towards the hollow tree.

Jimmy hauled out the suitcase. He grinned and started to get to his feet.

Rees froze.

"Man, hadn't you better take a look inside?" Jon said. "You never know. Someone might have beat you to it."

Jimmy knelt again, this time to open the suitcase. It was stuffed with packets of cocaine. He glanced at Jon and saw his gaze shift above him. His reaction was instinctive and immediate, he rolled to one side. The axe Rees held swung down, missing him.

Jimmy scrambled to his feet, unlooping the tomahawk from his shoulder. His other hand jerked the hunting knife from the trunk. Crouching, feet wide apart, he advanced on Rees.

Keeping his eyes on them, Jon struggled to get up from the ground. They were circling the tree trunk, feinting swings, out of reach of each other. Jon rolled over, face down, and forced himself onto his knees.

Jimmy had moved closer, within reach, tempting Rees. Rees chopped down at him. Jimmy sidestepped. The axe head missed, leaving Rees sprawled over the tree trunk.

Jimmy raised the tomahawk, swung it down. Jon on his feet whacked into him from behind. The blade dug deep into the wood. Jimmy tugged hard to free the weapon.

The axe flashed down at him.

Jimmy screamed and staggered back. With an arm pressed tight to his chest, he ran off wailing into the forest.

Rees cut Jon's wrists free with Jimmy's hunting knife. "Thanks, pal. You did good."

"You, too, bro."

Rees closed the suitcase, felt the weight in his hand. "We have got a shitload of coke here."

"Aren't we going after him?"

"Why? He won't be bothering us no more."

"No. I guess not."

The tomahawk, embedded in the tree trunk, was still clutched by Jimmy's severed hand.

***

Jason stopped pacing the cabin room. He gestured at the two girls, sitting with Muller at the dining table, a shrug of impatience. "Listen to me. I swear I had nothing to do with the killings." He sighed. "Why in hell would I have Raul killed? The guy was one of my best agents. An LA cop."

Karin stayed unmoved. "Yes, we both know about that."

"You do? Okay, then. What else do you know?"

Karin looked at Fara, uncertain of how much to tell him.

Fara frowned at Jason. "This whole thing, the reason you brought us over here, is so you can nab Jon with the coke."

"Sure. He was our only lead. But we are after the big boys, the heavy-duty cartel, not him." Jason turned to Muller. "I am worried about the kid. He will be top of their hit list."

Muller stirred in his seat. "Either of you gals got an idea where the boy might be right now?"

Fara looked at Karin.

"I think we should tell them," Karin said.

Fara turned to Jason. "Jon is showing the psycho where the stuff is hidden."

Jason wiped his brow. "Shit!"

The sheriff leaned forward. "Did the boy tell either of you gals where he hid the coke?"

Karin answered. "He said it would be safer if he didn't tell us."

"I guessed as much."

Jason sighed. "Muller, the moment the cartel know, they'll bury him."

"I reckon so." The sheriff rose from the table and went over to the window.

Karin smothered a gasp.

Jason sat down next to her. "What is bothering you, Karin?"

"Rees is out there with Jon."

"You hear that, Muller?" Jason's eyes returned to the girls. "For heaven's sake, why didn't you tell me all this before?"

Muller beckoned him. "Well, lookie here. It could be them a-coming."

Jason joined him at the window. Two figures were approaching. The sky had darkened into dusk, but he recognised them: Eileen and Sam.

He saw Eileen halt, heard her call. "Sam! Over there!" She had seen Raul's corpse on the porch. They were standing over the body when he reached them. "Is that Raul?" she asked.

"Yeah." He put an arm around her. "Leem is dead, too."

"Leem?"

Sam gave a cackle. "Heck, any of them kids still left alive?"

Jason felt Eileen tense herself in anticipation. "The girls are in the cabin with Sheriff Muller," he told her.

"Thank god."

"How about the others?" Sam asked. "Them two boys."

"I wish I knew. They are out there somewhere."

Eileen jerked herself free of him. "Do you mean you don't know where they are?"

Sam grunted. "Lady, finding them won't be no problem. I spotted their tracks way back." He straightened. "It's okay. Me and Mr Bligh here will bring them in. Safe and sound."

"No. I'm coming with you."

Jason intervened. "He is right, Eileen. Stay with the girls. They need you."

They waited on the porch until the cabin door closed behind her. "Is that your whirlybird, Mr Bligh," Sam asked, "sat over there?"

"Yeah. What do you need?"

"Torches, I guess. And maybe a couple of rifles if you have them. Just in case."

"No problem."

They climbed into the passenger area of the helicopter. Jason switched on the overhead lights.

"The rifles are back there. I'll get us the torches. We keep two in the cockpit up front."

The cockpit was in semi-darkness, a glimmer of light coming through from the passenger area. The first aid cabinet was wide-open, plasters and bandages scattered on the seats. Jason frowned and reached for his revolver. A hand gripped his wrist, an arm closed around his throat. Jimmy had risen, unseen, behind him.

The pair lurched out of the cockpit, Jason struggling to free himself. Sam watched them impassively. He was holding a rifle. "Jimmy, ain't you through killing people yet?"

Jimmy's arm tightened, the biceps muscle bulging. The crack of breaking vertebrae signalled the end. Jason's lifeless body slumped to the floor.

Sam crouched. "Darned if the feller ain't easier to take to, now that he ain't talking none."

Jimmy moaned and showed his stump. "Sam. Look what they done to me."

"Yeah, I seen it. Guess you won't be shooting them bows and arrows no more." He cackled and picked up Jason's revolver. "Maybe this will come in handy."

TEN: RETRIEVAL

To begin with they took turns carrying the suitcase, it was heavy and cumbersome, while the other led the way. But when the sky darkened, Rees lost sight of the path and told Jon to lead the way. "All I can see is trees."

"City people don't have a sense of direction. Or so they tell me."

"Where are you from then?"

"Downtown LA."

Their pace slowed. Jon lost the trail from time to time but managed to pick it up later. They were off trail when they heard a metallic click. A torch beam picked them out. They halted blinded by the glare.

The shadowy figure holding the torch cackled. "You boys put me in mind of a couple of scared jack rabbits."

Rees felt his heart thud. "Sam? Is that you?"

"If it ain't me, I got no idea who else it might be."

The torch beam rested momentarily on the suitcase Rees was holding, then lifted again.

"Quit blinding us, will you?" Jon said.

"Just making sure you got what you came out here for." Sam lowered the torch and walked towards them. A rifle was strapped across his back. "Me and that English lady has been looking all over for you kids."

Rees's heartbeat quickened again. "Miss Porter? She's alive?"

"Sure was, the last time I seen her."

"Where was that?" Jon asked.

"In a log cabin. Keeping company with them pair of gals you left behind."

"Did they tell you what has been going on?"

"Some." Sam lifted the torch beam up to the suitcase. "Reckon it must be the cocaine you got in there."

"Do you want to take a look?"

"Heck, no, we ain't got time for that. Them women are all back in the cabin, a-waitin' for the both of you." Sam turned away. "Plain worried sick."

Rees and Jon followed him.

**

For an hour or more Eileen sat at the table hearing the two girls tell her what had happened since she and Sam were swept away down river. Listening to them, watching them, she was aware that their manner towards each other had changed, exactly as she had hoped and expected. They had become close, two friends, loyal and respectful to one another.

All the same, she had the impression that they were holding something back, as if they regarded her as untrustworthy. Leem's death had shocked her most of all, but neither of them would give her any details and, acting together, had blocked her way when she tried to enter the bedroom.

At the end of their account Eileen got up from the table and went over to Muller at the window. "Any sign of them?"

"Not yet."

"Sheriff, are you aware that Mr Bligh is a policeman?"

"Is that right?"

"The girls think he is after a gang of drug traffickers."

"Yeah. They said."

Eileen peered through the window at the dark shape of Jason's helicopter on the far edge of the clearing. Her eyes narrowed. There was a glow coming from the cockpit. "That's very odd. The helicopter lights are on."

Muller glanced through the window. "I guess we forgot to switch them off, Miss Porter."

His answer aroused her suspicion, she seemed to recall an unlit shape on the clearing. "That's unlike Mr Bligh."

"Me, too." Muller said. He saw her start towards the cabin door. "Hey, where do you think you are going?"

Eileen halted. "Out there, to the helicopter." She searched for an innocent reason. "It's the lights, the ones which you and Mr Bligh left on. They might flatten the battery."

Muller chuckled. "Lady, it ain't a twelve-volt they got powering that chopper."

"You will probably think me silly, sheriff, but I would feel happier if I turned them off."

Muller came towards her. "Well, I'd like it a whole lot better if you stayed put. There is a dangerous killer on the loose out there." He took hold of her arm. "And since I am the only lawman this side of San Petro, and you folk are my responsibility, you are gonna have to do like I ask."

"Yes, of course, sheriff."

Karin went to the window. She saw Sam step out of the forest into the clearing. "Miss Porter, they are back."

Eileen shook herself free and turned for the cabin door again.

Muller drew the revolver from his holster. "Like I just said, lady. You ain't going

nowhere." He waggled the gun at Karin. "Both of you, go sit at the table, where I can see you all."

***

Rees and Jon followed Sam out of the forest. Rees saw the helicopter. He lowered the suitcase. "Why didn't you tell us Mr Bligh was here?"

"Plumb forgot." Sam cackled. "I guess you kids will be going back to prison

in style."

Jon glowered. "Not with that creep. All he's after is the fucking coke, man."

"Course he is. He's a cop, ain't he?"

"What about the killings?" Rees asked. "Leem and Raul?"

"Are you sayin' he did them?"

"No, I'm not, Raul was his choice, a copper." Rees paused and glanced at Jon. "Look, we think he was pulling the strings."

Sam grunted. "Never did take to the feller." He released the rifle safety catch and turned towards the helicopter. "Let's go ask him."

"How do you know he's in there, and not in the cabin with the others?" Jon asked.

"The lights are on, ain't they?"

They followed Sam to the helicopter, climbing aboard through the passenger door. It was semi-dark inside, the lights they saw were up front in the cockpit. Sam's voice was a whisper. "You two stay right here. Don't move till you hear me give a shout."

They watched his shadowy figure move forward to the cockpit. Jon kept his voice low. "I don't like this, pal."

"Me neither. Let's get back to the cabin."

The lighting brightened. Sam was framed in the doorway of the cockpit. "Come on up, boys. Mr Bligh wants to see the both of you. He's got some talkin' to do."

Rees looked at Jon. He nodded but shook his head when Rees reached for the suitcase by the entry door. The pair made their way forward, Rees in the lead. Sam moved aside to let them by.

Rees stepped warily into the cockpit. The sight made him gasp. "Shit!" Jason's corpse was strapped into the pilot seat. Jimmy, in the co-pilot seat, was glaring up at him malevolently, holding a revolver.

Jon raised his voice. "Sam, you got it wrong. Mr Bligh is in no mood to speak to anyone."

"Reckon not." Sam let out a cackle. "Lately, he ain't been none too talkative." He sighed. "No reason, though, why you two shouldn't get yourselves nice and comfy."

"Both seats are taken, man."

"Heck, there's plenty more down here." Sam backed down the aisle. "How about them two?" He indicated two seats with his rifle.

Jimmy prodded Jon and Rees into them with Jason's handgun.

"You won't be needing that," Sam said, and took the hunting knife from Rees's belt. He levelled the rifle again. "Go get me some rope, Jimmy."

"Where from?"

"Last time I looked they kept a coil or two back there at the rear."

Jon waited until they were alone with Sam. "I should have known. You were the guy tracking me."

"You stole my property, son. I ain't a feller who takes kindly to that." He gave a shrug. "Don't matter none now though. I got it back."

"Yeah? Is that what you reckon?"

Sam frowned and waited for Jimmy to come back with a coil of rope. He propped the rifle. "Keep your gun on them."

"Where are you going?"

"To take a peek."

Sam squatted by the suitcase and emptied out the contents, a muddy mix of earth, twigs and leaves scraped up from the forest floor. He raised his head to look at Jon. "What do you call this?"

"A pile of shit. Isn't that what you've been looking for?"

Sam picked up his rifle. He aimed the barrel at Rees's chest. "You want I should shoot your friend?"

"Fuck you," Rees said. "You are going to kill us both anyway."

"There is far worse than just plain dying." Sam lowered the rifle. "Jimmy, they try anything, shoot them."

***

A knock on the cabin door alerted the sheriff. He drew his revolver. "Stay where you are." He was sitting at the table with the others, facing Eileen with Fara and Karin on either side.

Another knock. "Open up. It's me."

Muller holstered the gun before sliding the bolt open. The door swung wide, and Sam stepped through, rifle in hand. "Is there a problem, Sam?" he asked.

"A small one." Sam's gaze shifted to the table. "We need them two." He indicated Fara and Karin with his rifle.

The sheriff grinned. "You are saying those two young ones?"

"Yeah, that's right."

Muller went over to them. "You heard him. On your feet, gals."

Karin and Fara got up from the table. Eileen stepped in front of them. "You will have to shoot me first, you fat pig."

Muller snarled and raised his fist.

"Leave the woman be," Sam said. He grunted. "I'll say one thing, lady. You sure got plenty guts." He motioned at Muller. "Shut her in back."

Muller grabbed Eileen around the neck. She struggled to free herself. Both girls moved to help her. A warning shot from Sam into the floor made them shrink back.

Muller forced Eileen into the bedroom and bolted the door. "All done, Sam."

"Not yet, I'm gonna need your help with these two. Jimmy has had himself a little accident."

Karin faced them. "You are evil, the worst kind."

Sam shrugged. "That's as maybe." He aimed the rifle. "Either way, the next one is gonna spoil your pretty looks."

The sheriff shoved the two girls forward. Sam followed them across the clearing and into the helicopter.

Muller led the way into the passenger area. Jimmy had his back to him, the revolver trained on the two youngsters. "Sam said you had a little accident."

Jimmy moaned and raised his other arm.

"Shit, that is no accident."

Jimmy uttered a sob.

Sam cackled. "Heck, feller, we ain't come empty-handed. We got a present for you."

Jimmy turned and saw the two girls.

"Not yet awhile Jimmy." Sam gave another cackle. "The sheriff needs to tie up a few loose ends."

Muller reached out for the knife in Sam's belt. "Chief, I could do with that hunting knife of yours."

"Take it I don't want it no more,' Jimmy said, his eyes still on Karin.

Sam, cradling his rifle, waited until Muller finished tying Rees and Jon into their seats. "All done?"

Muller nodded.

Sam prodded Karin forward with his rifle. "Jimmy, you got a real treat coming." He cackled. "Allowing you can manage her single-handed."

Jimmy grinned. "Watch me." He tore open Karin's shirt. She struggled with him. Fara tried to help. Jimmy hit her hard in the stomach.

Rees groaned. "How can you do that to her?"

Jon looked at Sam. "Tell him to lay off."

"Hold it, Jimmy." Sam crouched over Jon. "Okay. I am listening, boy."

"We put the coke back."

"Back where?"

"Back where it was. Ask Jimmy."

"He give you a hand?" Sam cackled and looked up at Jimmy. "You know where he means?"

"Yeah." Jimmy glowered. "That's if he ain't lying."

"It's there all right," Rees said. "If you don't believe us, take a look."

Muller gestured impatiently. "They are playing for time, Sam."

"Well, they ain't getting any. We'll pick up the coke when we're done here." He turned to Jimmy. "Go get the other cop."

A little later Jimmy returned with the body of Raul over his shoulder. By then Muller had tied the two girls into their seats. He dumped Raul next to Karin and Muller strapped the seatbelts to hold the corpse in position.

Sam checked the teenagers one by one, pulling at the knotted ropes, making sure they were tied securely. "These here whirly-birds can get kind of bumpy." He cackled. "Especially when the pilot ain't exactly in his prime no more."

Muller watched him with a sour expression. "That meet with your taste?" he said at the end.

Sam gave another cackle. "Like chickens ready for roasting. Okay. Start her up." He turned to Jimmy. "I'll fetch the lady, you bring along the dead one."

They climbed down from the helicopter and headed for the cabin. A few paces short of the cabin door Jimmy halted, a frown on his face. "Are we gonna need all of the dead one, Sam?"

"Reckon we do. What are you getting at, Jimmy?"

Jimmy grinned and turned away to the side wall of the log cabin. Sam followed him along the wall to the rear of the cabin.

Jimmy bent down, reached into a hole and brought out the severed head of Leem. "Lucky I remembered, Sam."

"Always knew you'd keep a cool head." Sam started a cackle but stopped short. His eyes narrowed. "Is that hole a tunnel into the bedroom?"

Jimmy gave a nod. Yeah, I put it there just in case..."

Sam raised his rifle and fired a warning shot. "Goddam! The lady could be loose."

***

An instant before the sheriff closed the bedroom door, Eileen caught sight of a cigarette lighter. She stood unmoving in the darkness until her eyes adapted to the candle glow filtering in through the frame of the doorway. Long enough for her to make out the outline of Leem's headless body on the bed. Kneeling at the edge, reaching underneath, her fingers encountered the cigarette lighter.

A click and the flame came on, small and wavering. She used the flame to light the stub of a candle. With her back turned to the bed, desperately avoiding sight of the corpse, her eyes circled the room. The walls were windowless and blank apart from the door that faced her. The only sound to be heard was her own panting. She was alone in the cabin.

Her attempts to force the door open were to no avail, the outside bolt stayed firmly in place. At length she raised the candle high. The log roof was beyond her reach even if she tried standing on tiptoe on the bed. Lowering the flame, she noticed there were muddy footprints on the planked floor. With her gaze averted, she heaved the bed away from the wall exposing an opening in the planks, a tunnel.

She crawled through on her elbows, holding the candle. The flame flickered. Looking up she saw Leem's severed head, his eyes wide and staring. Horrified, she blew out the candle and pushed hard. An inrush of fresh air. She had reached the end of the tunnel. It led her out into the open a few feet beyond the rear of the cabin. She replaced the severed head face down, sealing the tunnel again.

After a few deep breaths of air, she tracked along the side wall to the porch and peered through the window. The cabin was deserted, they were all in the helicopter.

Eileen made her way through the forest, coming out on to the clearing several paces from the aircraft. She could hear the murmur of voices. Without any clear plan in mind, she drew closer, listening. Sam was speaking. "I'll fetch the lady, you bring along the dead one."

His words made Eileen take those final few steps to the helicopter.

Hidden in the shadow beneath the fuselage she watched two men cross the clearing to the cabin.

One was Sam carrying his rifle, the other a powerful figure, muscular and bare-breasted. Coming closer to the cabin he halted and turned to Sam. She recognised him, Jimmy Mohawk, the owner of the Red Buffalo diner. A revolver was stuffed in his belt.

Above her the helicopter engine started up. She stayed still and silent, uncertain of what to do next. Sam glanced back. Instead of entering the cabin through the door as she expected, the old man and the owner of the diner both disappeared around the side wall.

Eileen eased out of the shadow of the helicopter with her mind made up. The rotor blades had begun to turn overhead. There was only one man, the sheriff, inside and he was in the cockpit. He was armed but the element of surprise lay in her favour. She prepared herself to go in through the boarding entry and creep up on him from behind.

The teenagers saw her enter. They were tied into their seats in the passenger area. She started silently towards them. A rifle shot from the cabin made her halt, clearly it was a signal from Sam that she was missing. Her eyes scanned her surroundings. Turning, she saw a flare pistol within reach by the doorway.

A voice that she recognised sounded in her ear. "Lady, you are being one hell of a nuisance."

A picture of the Heronimo sheriff standing in the aisle by the cockpit, gun in hand, formed in her mind. She turned and fired in one movement. A scream as the rocket ploughed into Muller's midriff, the force knocking him backwards into the cockpit.

Unseen by her, Muller's body crashed into the pilot seat, causing Jason to tilt forward, his dead hand falling on the throttle control. The engine roared, the helicopter jerked forward and started to spin.

Eileen caught sight of Jimmy framed in the entry doorway, hanging on with his one good arm. She lurched up the aisle into the cockpit, stepped over Muller's body, and pushed Jason's hand down hard on the throttle. The helicopter whirled faster. An instant later, she saw Jimmy flash upwards past the windscreen and hit the ground twenty paces away, a lifeless heap.

Sam went over to him.

Eileen shoved Jason's body out of the way and sat down in the pilot's seat. She slowed the helicopter and brought it to a standstill, facing Sam head on.

"Muller?" he shouted. "Are you there?"

She stayed silent.

"Lady? Is that you?"

She waited. Her hand had moved to the throttle control.

He approached warily, aiming his rifle.

She pushed hard. "So long, old timer." The rotor blades speeded up.

Sam stopped and fired a shot, a split-second before the helicopter crunched into him. His aim was good, a tiny crack appeared at eye level in the bullet-proof glass windscreen.

She returned to the passenger area and freed Karin and Fara. "You two can manage the boys, can't you?"

Karin looked at Fara, and they both giggled. "Gee, I sure hope we can."

"How are we getting back, Miss Porter?" Rees asked.

She turned away. "In style."

"Let's untie Rees first," Fara said.

"Yeah," Karin agreed. "That sounds about right."

Jon waited for the two girls to free Rees. "My turn now."

Not yet," Karin said. "There is something we'd like to know."

"What might that be?"

Fara answered. "Are you going to tell us where the coke is hid?"

"I guess not, that would make you accomplices. But I'll confide that the both of you were sitting on a million bucks."

Fara frowned. "Do you mean on that hollow tree trunk?"

"Yeah. The two of you dying for a smoke."

"I sure could do with one now," Karin said.

"Me, too," Karin agreed.

Both sat down and watched Rees untie Jon.

They heard the clack of rotor blades.

"Does she know how to fly one of these, pal?" Jon wondered aloud.

Rees grunted. "Bro, I ain't never asked her."

Jon yawned. "I guess it's something we'll find out soon enough."

The helicopter began to rise. Karin clutched hold of Rees. "Gee, I sure hope she does know how."

Rees held her close. "Easy, girl. Miss Porter can manage anything she turns her hand to."

"Yeah, anything," Fara said and kissed Jon. "But not anybody."

The helicopter rose above the cabin, hovered, then zoomed off into the night sky.

Printed in Great Britain
by Amazon